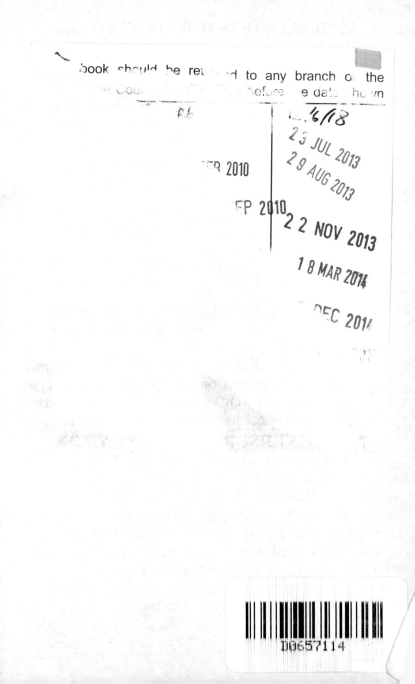

FOLLY TO LOVE

Lucy starts her new life with her uncle in Cornwall, unaware that she will stumble on some dangerous secrets. Innocently helping a poor family, she becomes enmeshed in treachery and murder, and discovers that her uncle is the leader of a smuggling gang. Lucy is attracted to Marcus Trenarren, a local land-owner, but suspects he may also be a smuggler ... It is only when her own life is in danger that she finds where her true happiness lies.

Books by Linda James
in the Linford Romance Library:

YIELD TO A TRAITOR
A JEALOUS HEART

LINDA JAMES

FOLLY TO LOVE

Complete and Unabridged

LINFORD
Leicester

First published in Great Britain in 2007

First Linford Edition
published 2008

British Library CIP Data

James, Linda
    Folly to love.—Large print ed.—
    Linford romance library
    1. Smuggling—England—Cornwall (County)
    —Fiction 2. Cornwall (England : County)
    —Fiction 3. Love stories 4. Large type books
    I. Title
    823.9'2 [F]

    ISBN 978–1–84782–150–8

Published by
F. A. Thorpe (Publishing)
Anstey, Leicestershire

Set by Words & Graphics Ltd.
Anstey, Leicestershire
Printed and bound in Great Britain by
T. J. International Ltd., Padstow, Cornwall

This book is printed on acid-free paper

1

The gale force wind buffeted the coach from Exeter relentlessly as it travelled along Bodmin Moor. Numerous times the vehicle swerved to try and avoid the potholes in the road. The sole occupant, Lucy Armitage, had been travelling from Yorkshire for five days and she clung on to the leather straps wishing she had never agreed to come to this wild bleak county of Cornwall.

The coachman, Watson, had assured her at their last stop they would reach Folly Cove, her destination, before nightfall, but already the light was fading, turning the bleak landscape to dark shadows. The large expanse of water they were just passing reflected darkness on its rippling surface from the leaden sky.

She was nearing journey's end and feeling increasingly nervous about meeting her mother's brother whom she had never met. Lucy's parents were now both dead and an unexpected offer of a home for her had arrived from Tobias Penmarick. In this year of 1814 being almost penniless and not having the means to make her own living, she'd had no option but to swallow her pride and reply to Uncle Tobias' letter, accepting his generous offer, for only when she attained the age of twenty-one would the inheritance from her late father's estate pass to her.

Her uncle was a widower, childless and living alone and she hoped he would be welcoming and not view her as an incumbrance. There had been an estrangement between her father and his brother-in-law, and as a consequence Uncle Tobias had severed all contact with his sister and her family several years before. The reason for the rift was apparently due to Tobias not being agreeable to his sister marrying a northern man and leaving Cornwall.

Lucy was deep in her reverie when

she realised the coach was coming to a halt. She leaned out and saw a rider approaching from the direction they were heading. The man reined in his horse alongside the coach.

'Wasn't expecting to see you this night, Squire,' Watson said with surprise in his tone.

'There's a change of plan, Watson. We'll need your assistance tonight. Go to the Tor Head and wait for instructions.'

Lucy was so intrigued by the conversation she didn't realise at first the man had turned his attention to her.

'Who is your passenger?' he asked.

'A Miss Armitage, heading for Tobias Penmarick's house near Folly Cove.'

'Is she indeed?' The rider nudged his horse nearer to the window where Lucy was watching him with interest. His studied gaze took in her chestnut curls escaping from the confines of her plain poke bonnet. In the fading light he could not determine the colour of her eyes and although she was no beauty, there was a delicate prettiness in her regular features.

Lucy returned the man's stare. Despite his plain homespun tailcoat and breeches, Lucy noted his hessian boots were of good quality polished leather. His voice was cultured and his manner authoritative.

'Do you know my uncle, sir?' she ventured to ask, beginning to feel ill at ease under his scrutiny.

'Tobias Penmarick is your uncle?'

'Yes, I am to live at his house, although I haven't met him before.'

The man frowned. 'Then I wish you well, Madam. Tobias Penmarick has a dour nature and is not known for his generosity.'

'He is being generous enough to provide me with a home until I come of age and obtain my inheritance.'

'You will find Cornwall harsh and bleak. Some don't welcome strangers,' he stated bluntly. 'I am not one of them. I hope you will settle at High

Ridge, Miss Armitage.'

'Cornwall is no bleaker than parts of my home county, Yorkshire. I'm used to wild rugged moors, but the people in my part of the world are on the whole friendly,' she rejoined tartly.

The man's expression was sardonic as he touched his hat in acknowledgement before moving away. There was a short conversation with Watson before he rode back the way he had come. Watson alighted from his high seat and checked the horses' harnesses.

'Who is that man?' Lucy asked, her gaze still on the rider.

'That be Marcus Trenarren, Miss. A landowner and well respected in these parts. I dare say you'll be seeing him around the area.' He glanced up at the stormy clouds. 'Can't go much further today, Miss. The weather's turning nasty. A few miles up this road there's a respectable hostelry. If you don't mind we'll be staying there over night. It'll give the horses a chance to rest.'

Mentioning the horses didn't give

Lucy much of an argument. Besides she was bone weary herself and had to trust the coachman's assertion the inn was respectable. She could do nothing but accept the situation.

Marcus Trenarren's conversation with Watson came to mind. He had told the coachman to go to the Tor Head, presumably the inn, and wait for instructions. What instructions she wondered? Would she have reached her destination that night if he had not appeared and intervened?

After what seemed an interminable time, the coach turned off the road and rumbled into the cobbled yard of the Tor Head inn. Helped by Watson, Lucy alighted from the vehicle and stared up at the ancient building with its granite slate roof and stone walls.

Watson led her down a passage into a warm cosy parlour with a fire roaring up the chimney. Low blackened beams supported the ceiling and the floor was stone flagged. He indicated she seat herself on the settle near the fire.

'You'll be comfortable here, Miss Armitage,' he informed her. 'The beds are clean and the food's good.'

Several men, sitting at the tables hushed their conversation, all eyes turning to her. Watson vanished and she was left alone to face their curious stares. There was one man staring at her more intently than the others. He was young, perhaps a year or two older than herself. His expression was insolent, as he scrutinised her from head to foot.

A young girl appeared, carrying a large tray full with tankards. She swayed towards the man's table and set down the tray with such a clatter, the ale spilled over in pools of froth on to the tray. The man spoke to the tavern maid, his eyes still on Lucy. The girl nodded and moved away to serve the other customers, then she sauntered over to Lucy.

'What would you like, Miss?'

Lucy gave the girl her request, still conscious of the man's eyes on her.

'Who is that man, sitting near the

door? He has not stopped staring since I walked in!'

'Take no notice of him, Miss. He's always curious about strangers. Just plain nosy I call it,' she said in a soft Cornish dialect. 'That's Jack Malvern. We're walking out together. Have you much farther to travel?' she asked pleasantly.

'I'm not sure.' Lucy replied. 'I'm travelling to a place called Folly Cove near Falcombe. My uncle lives there and has invited me to stay with him. His house is called High Ridge and is built close to the cliffs.'

The woman's smile faded. 'Your uncle must be Tobias Penmarick. Didn't know he had kin. I'm afraid your uncle is not liked in these parts. Too friendly with the gibbet, that's what he is,' she remarked, walking away. She stopped to whisper to Jack Malvern.

Lucy began to feel a twinge of apprehension. Marcus Trenarren had also spoken somewhat detrimentally against her uncle.

The girl returned with hot soup and pasties. 'By the way, my name's Kate. I'll put a jug of hot water in your room when you're ready to retire. In the morning I'll knock on your door about seven. Watson said the coach leaves at eight.'

Lucy thanked her. She began to eat her supper, relieved when Jack Malvern got up and went out.

Later the landlord's wife showed her to an adequately furnished upstairs room overlooking the stable. The wind battered at the casement and spots of rain began to beat against the window-pane. Lucy eased her feet out of her shoes and removed her coat. She inspected the counterpane and sheets for cleanliness, nodding to herself approvingly, then moved to the jug and basin provided. After a quick all over wash she took her nightgown from the large travel bag she had brought with her.

Below in the stable yard, there was

the sound of a horse's hooves clattering on the cobbles. Lucy didn't take much notice at first and donned her night attire, anxious to retire after such a gruelling journey. Then she heard Watson's voice.

Curiosity got the better of her and she snuffed the candle before peering out. In the light from the lantern fixed to the stable wall, Lucy could see the coach driver was in conversation with Marcus Trenarren. After a minute or so the pair moved into the inn out of sight.

She moved away from the window and got into bed, thinking no more of the two men. The bedding smelled of fresh lavender and within minutes she fell into a dreamless sleep. It was the insistent rapping on the door which finally roused her. She opened her eyes to see it was daylight.

'Are you awake, Miss? I've brought you some warm water to wash with.'

Lucy sat up and pushed her hair from her eyes. 'Yes, come in, Kate,' she called.

Kate entered looking bright and cheerful, causing Lucy to feel envious that the girl could be so alert that early in the morning.

'It's nearly seven. You'll be wanting to break your fast, I'm sure.' She set down the pail of warm water and without preamble opened the window and threw the dirty water Lucy had used the night before down into the yard.

'There's hot porridge and buttered muffins for breakfast, Miss, when you come down to the parlour.'

Lucy thanked her and after Kate had gone she had a thorough wash and dressed herself. The parlour was chilly when Lucy entered; the newly-lit fire not yet burned through to ward off the cold. Kate brought her porridge, then piping hot muffins from the oven with butter and jam to finish.

'The wind's dropped and there's a thick fog over the moor,' Kate said. 'You should reach High Ridge in about an hour or less.'

'I do hope so,' Lucy replied. 'I'm

most anxious to see my new home and meet my uncle.'

'Your uncle's house is in a bleak place, Miss. You might find it hard to settle. Lots of folk wouldn't live there.'

Lucy stared at her, but Kate didn't elaborate before she walked away. She was beginning to wonder just what was awaiting her?

The coach manoeuvred out of the inn yard at precisely eight o'clock. Fog enshrouded the landscape and at regular intervals strange standing stones and Celtic crosses loomed into view. The road curved and the horrifying sight of a gibbet on a crossroads could be seen. Thankfully no-one was hanging from it, then a minute later the coach came to a halt.

Watson threw Lucy's travel bag on to the ground and climbed down. 'Here you are, Miss Armitage,' he said opening the door and helping her out. 'That be High Ridge over there.'

Lucy gazed to where he pointed. She could barely see anything in the fog which was thickening by the minute. The grey outline of a building was just visible on a high vantage point. The house was built in such a way it seemed to rise up as part of the rocks itself. The sea below growled and thundered against the rocks making a loud booming sound.

'It's not far to walk, Miss Armitage. There's a gate over there then you'll see the steps leading up to the house.'

She gave him the fare and thanked him. As the two horses began to move, taking the coach away, Lucy felt a twinge of fear. She was going into the unknown and her courage was beginning to desert her. Chiding herself for her foolishness she began to walk in the direction Watson had indicated.

After some minutes and not having reached the gate, Lucy realised she must have missed it. She could hardly see a hand before her and the house was now completely obliterated. The sound of the sea was nearer and she stopped for a moment, trying to get her bearings.

She began to walk on again then realised she was walking down a wide track when she should be heading upwards. She could hear voices and just had a minute to realise the sea was below, when seconds later three men appeared out of the fog, dragging a rowing boat up the slope. As they got nearer, Lucy recognised one of them as Jack Malvern, Kate's sweetheart.

'Well, I never, it's the fine little lady come to live with our friend up there.' Jack Malvern's bold gaze slid over her slight form and the travel bag clutched in her hand. 'Why are you wandering about down here in this pea souper? You wouldn't have seen anything unusual would you, Miss?' He moved closer, searching her features.

'I would be hard put to see anything in this weather, let alone anything unusual,' she answered in a sharp tone.

Jack stared at her for a moment, seemingly deep in thought. 'You're a fine looking woman,' he mused. 'If I wasn't walking out with Kate . . . ' His hand touched her cheek.

She backed away, causing him to grin.

'There's nothing to fear from me. Come on, I'll take you to Tobias.' He took the bag from her grasp and began to walk up the slope. She followed and a minute later they reached the gate. Narrow, steep stone steps were cut into the hillside. There was no handrail and as they climbed higher Lucy had to stop a moment as a wave of dizziness attacked her. She wondered, with a feeling of dread if this was the sole access to High Ridge. Jack sprinted out of sight, but he was waiting for her at the top.

Seeing her expression he laughed rather cruelly as if aware of her aversion to heights.

'Wait until the fog lifts and you can see the whole area and the sea below.'

'No thank you,' she muttered. 'Is there no other way to reach this house?'

'Don't you worry, little lady. This is the back of the house. There's a driveway at the front. I expect Watson was in a hurry. That's why he dropped you on the gibbet road.'

Lucy expelled her breath in relief. Trying to forget the hair-raising steps, she stared up at her new home. The house was much larger than she imagined, but it had a brooding neglected aura with squat, square windows and no curtains to soften the bleak façade.

'Like the look of it, do you, Miss?' Jack was studying her expression.

'It appears rather daunting,' she murmured. 'Very different to my home in Yorkshire.'

'You'll get used to it,' he said. 'Here comes your welcoming party. One word of warning. There are strange goings on in these parts. If you hear noises in that house take no notice. The sea runs partly into caves under the house at high tides. Its best to ignore anything you hear. That way you keep safe.' With that he quickly descended the steps and was gone.

Lucy turned to see a man standing in a doorway, watching her. He neither spoke or moved forward in greeting. She felt a nervous flutter as she picked up her bag and walked towards the motionless figure.

No sign of friendly greeting lit the man's sallow features, but there was no doubting this was her uncle. The family resemblance was too marked.

'Good day, Uncle Tobias. I'm Lucy Armitage, your niece.' She held out her hand which was ignored.

'You should have arrived yesterday,' he said sounding disgruntled. He turned abruptly and walked into the house. Following his tall thin frame down a long passage she felt totally unwelcome. She wanted to fling this man's invitation in his face and return home, but she couldn't. She had to stay in this bleak place with its reticent master!

2

Lucy followed her uncle across a stark hall, into a large room which was equally austere. The only furniture was a polished walnut table, four chairs and a settle placed near the fire. There was a distinct chill in the air and Lucy tried to refrain from shivering.

Tobias indicated she seat herself on the settle. Lucy glanced around at the curtainless windows and bare floorboards. The room was devoid of any comfort, not even a rug and the fire was flickering feebly, on the point of dying out for want of fuel.

'Do you need food?' Tobias spoke in a sharp tone. He had placed himself with his back to the fire, depriving Lucy of what little warmth there was.

'Thank you, Uncle, but I ate at the Tor Head Inn barely an hour ago.'

'Well, perhaps some mulled wine?' He moved to the side of the mantelpiece and pulled a bell rope.

'That would be lovely, I am rather cold,' she replied. 'The delay in my arriving was due to the gales last evening,' she explained.

'There's no need to explain. I guessed as much.' He subjected her to a fixed stare. 'Was your journey from Yorkshire comfortable?' He appeared ill at ease as though his enquiry was a mere formality to get through and not a genuine desire to welcome her.

'Not altogether, Uncle. Many of the roads are in a poor state and I suffer greatly from travel sickness.'

'Well, it is over now, you are here. I offered you a home for the sake of your mother's memory. I would not see her daughter bereft of a home.' He halted and clamped his lips tightly as if he was overcome with emotion.

'May I ask why you did not attend the funeral?'

'I am not a well man. Your mother

and I have had no contact for several years.'

'Yes, I am aware of that, but she was your sister!'

'No more questions!' he snapped. 'If you wish to remain in a happy state here it is better if you keep your own counsel. Did your mother tell you anything about High Ridge?'

'Only its location and that it has been in our family for two hundred years.'

'You will not find this a comfortable house, but one day it will be yours,' he announced unexpectedly. 'As I have no heirs, you are the next in line. Whether you will want the place after you have lived here a few months is debatable. This is a harsh place. We are open to all the elements being in such an elevated position. My wife, Penelope, found it intolerable in winter. The reason for her early death, I'm certain.'

'Truly, I had not expected to be your heir,' she said, totally surprised. 'Perhaps you will marry again?'

Tobias was still a relatively young

man. By Lucy's calculations he must still only be in his forties. Although a little on the emaciated side he was quite distinguished looking with dark hair, greying at the temples.

'Marriage!' he spluttered in contempt. 'Marriage is for young fools! I have already named you in my will as my beneficiary. No more to be said.'

There was a knock on the door, followed by the entrance into the room of a slim, dark woman.

'Ha, here is Mrs Samuel, my housekeeper. This is my niece, Lucy Armitage.'

The woman murmured a greeting, but there was nothing welcoming in her expression. The eyes which swept over Lucy were like black coals in a face as white as the lace cloth she began to spread over the table. She was clothed from head to foot in black, relieved only by a pristine white lace collar.

A shiver ran down Lucy. She didn't know whether it was from the chilly room or the hostility in the housekeeper's eyes.

'Bring us some mulled wine, Elvira. I trust my niece's room is ready?'

'Of course it's ready!' She sent Tobias an indignant glare. Her darting shrewd eyes slid to Lucy again before she swept out of the room.

'You may find my housekeeper a little stern, but she means well,' Tobias said, at last moving from the fire and seating himself on one of the dining chairs.

'You may move about the house freely, but you will find some of the rooms are kept locked as they are not in use. The sea at high tide reaches far under the foundations of the house. At times you will hear the consequence of this, but do not be alarmed. If you go for a walk down to Folly Cove under no circumstances enter the caves, even when the tide is out. The tunnels are long and twisting. If you were trapped by the sea there is no other way out! Do I make myself clear?'

'Perfectly, Uncle. I will certainly heed your warning, but if the only way to the cove is down those hazardous steps then I doubt I will see the beach.'

'There is another way down to the cove and I shall ask Mrs Samuel to show you.' A ghost of a smile lifted his lips. 'I recall your mother didn't like those steps either when we were children. I'm afraid I used to tease her mercilessly and drag her down them.'

Lucy could imagine he would be rather cruel as some boys are. She didn't know him but her first impression was that he was not an immediately likeable person.

The housekeeper returned with a tray on which was a large pewter jug. She set the tray down and poured the dark red wine into two tankards.

'Is my niece's room aired properly, Elvira?' Tobias enquired.

Elvira scowled. 'Have I ever failed in my duties?' She appeared genuinely annoyed as she served them with the wine.

Tobias tutted. 'No, of course you haven't. You've served me loyally for several years now. I'm just ensuring you've lit a fire in my niece's room?'

'Yes, there's a roaring fire, a bed warmer, extra blankets and even rugs to keep her feet from the cold floors. Anything else, sir?' Elvira's tone was, to Lucy's hearing rather insolent for a servant.

'No, that will do, Elvira, thank you.'

'I can't be too stern with her.' Tobias remarked when she had gone. 'I rely on her greatly. If she left I couldn't manage on my own. That's why I ignore her less than servile manner.'

Lucy nodded, feeling the warmth of the mulled wine dispel some of the cold in her body.

'I regret I was not able to be of help after your father died. I was not in a position to help anyone I'm afraid. Suffered some business losses.' He didn't elaborate further.

Lucy sipped the pleasant tasting wine and was glad when he broke the uneasy silence by rising to his feet to pull the bell rope.

'Elvira will show you to your room

now. I'm sure you would like to acquaint yourself with your new home and relax until luncheon.'

'Yes, Uncle. Thank you for offering to give me a home with you. I am truly grateful and I will try to be as unobtrusive as possible.'

'I don't expect you to walk around like a mouse, but one thing, I am the local magistrate and when I am entertaining colleagues I would prefer it if you occupy yourself elsewhere.'

'Yes, I will, Uncle,' she murmured.

Elvira entered at that moment.

'Please show my niece to her room, now, Elvira.' The housekeeper made no comment and, picking up Lucy's travel bag, she walked from the room. Lucy was about to follow her.

'Before you go, please don't call me Uncle. I would much prefer Tobias,' he instructed.

'Very well, Un ... Tobias.' Lucy corrected herself. She hurried out of the room, after Elvira who was halfway up the wide staircase which must at one time been very elegant. The woodwork on the banister was unpolished and scratched and the stair carpet thread-bare. Tobias had hinted at having money problems and what she had seen so far of the house she guessed it needed quite a lot spending on it.

Already she had noticed damp patches on the walls and there was a severe shortage of basic furniture and furnishings. Surely as a magistrate he could not be in such dire straits?

She was pondering these things when she realised Elvira had reached the top of the stairs and disappeared around a corner, not waiting for her to catch up. Although she had just met the woman, Lucy sensed Elvira Samuel did not welcome her presence at High Ridge for some reason.

The house was a virtual warren of corridors with rooms leading off. Away from the windows it was dark and gloomy with portraits lining the walls, of ancestors staring out with stern or melancholy features.

She was certain she'd never find her way back downstairs as she followed Elvira's distant dark garbed figure. At last the housekeeper halted at a door and entered a room. When Lucy caught up she was pleasantly surprised by the aspect as she entered. Two large windows threw light into the room which was dominated by a magnificent four poster bed. Several rugs covered the floor and a cheerful fire burned in the grate. Red plush velvet curtains hung at the windows.

'What a lovely room!' Lucy exclaimed. 'I think I shall settle very well in here.'

Elvira turned from removing the bed warmer to stare at her. 'Maybe you will, maybe not. There is nothing at High Ridge for a young girl like you. It would have been better if you'd stayed in Yorkshire! You'll find Cornish ways hard to understand,' she said bluntly.

'My uncle has been kind enough to offer me a home at a very difficult time in my life. I'm sure I shall become used to your 'Cornish ways' given time!'

Lucy answered with acid in her tone. She was beginning to think the housekeeper voiced her opinion too much and she would not be intimidated by her.

Clearly Elvira did not like her retort by the darkness of her expression. 'That's as maybe,' she mumbled, moving to the door. 'Luncheon will be served in an hour in the parlour.'

She stopped in the open doorway and glared back at Lucy. 'By the way, the master insists on strict punctuality at mealtimes.' Her parting words hung coldly in the air after she had gone.

Lucy wasn't at all certain she could find her way back through the maze of corridors, but she wouldn't give this stern-faced woman the satisfaction of thinking she was useless. Did she resent having another person in the house because of the extra work it involved?

She began to take her belongings from her bag. The only other two gowns she possessed were a serviceable dark grey heavy linen and her only best one, a white muslin with tiny sprigs of roses on the low cut bodice, although she did not anticipate having an occasion to wear it in this bleak countryside.

She went across to the window to gain an idea of where her room was situated, but the fog was still very dense and she could see barely nothing of the landscape. There was a draught coming in through the window and she moved quickly away to sit in the chair near the fire. Why did Tobias deprive himself of the basic need of warmth in such bitter weather? Had he done it so she could benefit by having this fire herself?

Again she began to wonder if her uncle was in dire financial straits. The fire soon dispelled the cold in her body. She dozed off and awoke stretching slowly. She glanced at the small silver clock of her father's she had brought with her and realised an hour had almost passed. She rose to her feet and straightened her gown. A quick flick with the brush teased her hair into place and she was ready.

She hurried along the corridors, trying to remember certain things such as portraits, but it was several minutes before she at last emerged at the head of the staircase. Voices, raised in anger could be heard from below in the hall. There was a bend in the staircase and it was only as she rounded it and could clearly see the hall did she realise it was Marcus Trenarren in heated conversation with Tobias.

Marcus was impeccably attired and looked every inch the imperious landowner in dark green velvet tail coat, fawn pantaloons and polished hessian boots, pristine white lawn neck cloth and dark brown beaver hat held in his hand. His black hair curled around his face and neck with unruly abandonment. He was the most handsome man she had ever seen, but his tone sounded dictatorial and arrogant.

'You're a fool, man! I'll give you until noon tomorrow, then I demand an answer!'

'I must have more time than that! It's

impossible to obtain ... ' Tobias stopped speaking. He had become aware of Lucy, standing midway on the stairs, watching them with a puzzled expression. The heated argument hung in the air as she resumed her descent.

Tobias moved forward and took Lucy's hand to escort her down the remaining two steps. 'This is my niece, Lucy Armitage from Yorkshire, my sister, Helen's daughter. Since both her parents have passed on, I have invited my niece to stay here for as long as she wishes. My dear, Marcus Trenarren of Craghill Hall, our local landowner.'

Marcus bent low over her hand. 'It is a pleasure to meet you, Miss Armitage. I hope you settle at High Ridge and Folly Cove.'

He did not remark on their meeting of the previous evening and the slight shake of his head, gave Lucy a warning that he wished it to remain secret between them.

'I am pleased to make your acquaintance, Mr Trenarren. Thank you for your welcome.' She felt a tremor run through her body as his steady gaze took in her clear grey eyes and pale skin. She silently chided herself for this silly foolishness.

'I look forward to our next meeting, Miss Armitage,' he said, moving to the outer door.

'Think seriously long and hard on what I have proposed.' He addressed Tobias before flinging open the door and leaving.

Lucy was still staring at the closed door through which Marcus Trenarren had gone when she realised Tobias was waiting for her to enter the parlour with him. As they took their places at the table, Lucy mulled over what she had heard. It sounded very much like Marcus was making veiled threats against Tobias. He had mentioned earlier to her he had suffered some losses. Was he in debt and owed Marcus money?

Whatever trouble Tobias was in, the meal was plain, but substantial. There was deliciously tender boiled beef, baby carrots and turnip with creamed potatoes. To follow was plum pudding and a rich sauce, flavoured with brandy.

'Did you overhear much of the conversation between Marcus and myself,' he suddenly asked while they were enjoying a second glass of claret after the meal.

'Very little, Tobias,' she said truthfully.

He was watching her reaction closely. 'Whatever you did hear, just forget it. Marcus Trenarren's father and myself were old enemies until he died a few months ago. It appears the son wants to carry the feud on. A warning, my dear. Marcus has a bad reputation with the ladies, steer well clear of him!'

'I'm sure he would not be interested in me, but it is another warning I shall heed.' Lucy began to believe there were unpleasant undercurrents at High Ridge she was just becoming aware of. How many more warnings was she to receive in this strange place?

3

Tobias announced he was riding into Falcombe and would be gone most of the afternoon. 'The fog appears to be lifting,' he remarked. 'Ask Elvira if she has time to show you around the gardens and the less perilous way down to Folly cove.'

'Yes, thank you, Tobias. If she is too occupied I shall explore myself. Have a good afternoon.'

Tobias' forehead creased in a frown. 'I have to attend court. Smugglers have been apprehended and caught. It's my task to see they can no longer get up to their notorious dealings. No doubt the hangman will help me rid this area of such vermin!'

Lucy shivered. Not just at the expression of smug satisfaction on his face, but the image of the gibbet not far from the house on the bleak crossroads.

She was well aware of the smuggling trade, such activities went on in her county along the coast. Even so she was hard pressed to believe they deserved to die for the crime. For many it kept body and soul together when there was no other employment.

Later, Lucy went to seek out Elvira and found her in the kitchen. There was a large, imposing cooking range and a surprisingly well-banked fire roared up the chimney.

Sitting at the table was a plump middle-aged woman. She had a pleasant expression and smiled as Lucy entered. Elvira was slipping a cloak over her shoulders. Her lips tightened at the sight of Lucy. 'Yes, Miss Armitage?'

'I was about to ask if you would show me the long way down to Folly Cove, but I see you are about to go out.'

'Why do you want to go walking about in this weather?' She didn't look too pleased.

'The fog is lifting. It doesn't matter, I can go another day.'

'It's my half day. Molly here fills in for me. If you're bent on going, she'll show you.' Elvira glared at Molly. 'Don't be too long. There's the master's dinner to prepare and that list of other jobs I've left for you. I'll be back early in the morning.' She turned to Lucy.

'Molly sleeps over for the night. She'll see to anything you need.' With that she swept out.

Molly rose to her feet and walked stiffly to the fire. She poured boiling water from the large blackened kettle into the brown earthenware teapot she was holding.

'Are you the master's relative come to stay?' she asked in a friendly tone.

'I'm Tobias' niece, Lucy Armitage. He has kindly invited me to live here for as long as I wish.'

'Welcome to High Ridge, Miss Armitage. I'm sure you'll love it here.'

Lucy smiled. 'Well, I believe you are the first person who has said that. Everyone else has only spoken doom and gloom, warning me about this and that.'

Molly poured the tea into cups and handed one to Lucy. They seated themselves in the two padded chairs on either side of the fire.

'Things are not as they were at High Ridge. It's since Mrs Penmarick passed on. There was always laughter in this house when she was here.' Her expression was far away for a second. 'I worked here for many years before my husband said I was getting too old to do all the skivvying. Now once a week suits me fine.'

'Why does Mrs Samuel have such a miserable countenance?'

'She always has. Maybe cos she's lost two husbands. Just had a baby when her first husband died of fever. Second was hung for smuggling.'

'I can have some sympathy for her then.' Lucy murmured.

Molly wrinkled her nose in distaste. 'Don't excuse her rude manner though, does it.' Molly stirred her tea slowly, deep in thought. 'Same with your uncle. He was always such a pleasant man . . . '

'Grief can do strange things to people.' Lucy murmured. She suspected from what she'd deduced already, it perhaps was not just her aunt's passing which was the cause for Tobias' dour nature. It was becoming apparent he had other serious pressing problems.

'When you've finished your tea I'll show you the path down to the cove.' Molly said a little while later.

'Oh, don't let me keep you from your tasks. I'm sure I can find the way.'

'Oh, don't you fret. I've plenty of time to get the work done. It won't take long. You go get your things and meet me here.'

Lucy found her room quicker than she anticipated and donned her thick long cloak and bonnet. Molly was ready in the kitchen and they set off down a stone flagged passage.

Lucy noticed there was another passageway leading off to the right with a door at the end. 'Where does that lead, Molly?' she asked.

'To the cellars, Miss. Master keeps it locked. His store of spirits is down there, if there's any left.'

'Well he must have some left. We had a nice glass of claret with our luncheon. I have noticed the house is sparsely furnished.'

'A lot of items have disappeared in the last few months. I don't like to think what it could mean.' Molly said, shaking her head.

After the snippet of conversation she heard earlier, Lucy was almost certain her uncle was in debt and Marcus Trenarren had some involvement in it.

They left the house by a side door into a spacious garden with well kept lawns, encircled by a high wall. There was an iron gate in the wall and Molly reached up to take down a large key hanging on a hook.

'When you return, don't forget to lock the gate again,' she instructed. 'The master likes to keep this gate locked. Don't know why, anyone can get into the grounds by the Folly steps.'

'I became lost in the fog and Jack Malvern showed me the way up those steps to the house.'

Molly turned to look at her. 'Jack Malvern, you say? He's Elvira's son by her first marriage and one to be avoided. I won't say anymore, but don't have anything to do with him.'

'I don't intend to, Molly. He was with some other men and they seemed suspicious of me.'

Molly gave her a thoughtful look. 'Take my advice, Miss Armitage. If you see anything out of the ordinary round these parts, turn a blind eye.' She unlocked the gate and it opened with a protesting creak. 'The path slopes gently down and leads straight on to the beach. There'll be afternoon tea at four.' She hung the key back on the hook. 'Enjoy your walk.'

Lucy set off and although she was high up the path was wide. Far in the distance, set back from the cliffs was a large imposing looking house, much grander than High Ridge and now the mist was clearing the whole of the bay could be seen in a wide beautiful arch.

She reached the beach in no time and walked towards the waters edge. The tide was well out, leaving a wide expanse of sand. She began to walk in the direction that took her past the house, perched high up on the cliff.

Ahead she could hear men's voices calling to each other, but couldn't see anyone as the cliff face jutted out, obscuring her view. Then she noticed the wide ridge in the sand. Someone had been dragging a boat up the beach. She followed the trail with her eyes and saw it led into what looked like an opening in the rock. She glanced up. The house was directly above, on the highest point of the headland.

She walked towards the mouth of the cave. There were footprints all around the opening. Were smugglers using this cave to hide things in? She had to bend her head to enter the cave. There was the boat, but where were the men who had brought it here? The light was dim, but she could just make out a tunnel and suddenly realised there were voices afar off coming nearer. She froze for a second. She had to hide! There was just time to retreat into the darkest corner of the cave.

'Mr High and Mighty can say all he likes, but I ain't about to risk my neck. There's a Riding Officer sniffing about in the area,' one of the men complained.

'You want as much of the rewards as we do, but won't do any of the dirty work!' Another man replied angrily.

'Do you want to hang on that gibbet? Penmarick would tie the rope around our necks himself if he thought it would save his own skin!' The first man replied.

'Aw, come on you two! Get this boat afloat. If we don't do the job we don't get paid and I for one want food in me belly!'

Lucy recognised Jack Malvern's voice. She hardly dare breathe as they began to drag the boat out of the cave. Only when they had gone did she exhale properly, but even so she waited several minutes. She eventually crept to the opening. The three men were well away from the shore, rowing hard, but she dare not emerge until they were out of sight.

There was no doubt they were smugglers, but what did they mean by the statement her uncle would hang them himself if he thought it would save his own skin? Surely he could not be a smuggler! He was a respected magistrate, a supposed pillar of the community.

★　★　★

Sometime during the night, Lucy awoke suddenly. She sat up, wondering where she was for a few seconds, then she became aware of a far off reverberating sound deep below the house. The noise was like the thunder she remembered as a child, when it rolled across the countryside getting nearer and nearer until it reached a crescendo overhead in a mighty thunderclap.

She slipped out of bed and went to the window. The tide was out, the moon casting a pale light on the white edged foam of the sea as it gently lapped the shore. If the sea wasn't making the noise, what was? She was just about to move away when she caught a flash of light out on the sea. It was waving to and fro as if someone was signalling to the shore.

Lucy watched for several minutes until the light disappeared. She got back into bed, shivering with the cold and lay for a long time listening to the strange noise. Eventually she fell asleep and the next thing she knew someone was knocking on her door.

'Morning, Miss Armitage. Did you sleep well?' Molly entered carrying a breakfast tray. She placed it on the small table near Lucy's bed.

Lucy pushed herself into a sitting position. 'Not very well, Molly. A noise kept me awake. At first I thought it was the sea running into the caves, but the tide was out. Did you hear it?'

Molly began to busy herself cleaning out the fire grate. 'No, Miss. I don't hear a thing once my head touches the pillow.'

She began to eat the porridge provided and watched as Molly lit the fire with bits of wood and paper, waiting until there were enough flames to place two small logs on top.

'Won't be long before it warms the room, Miss.' She struggled to her feet. 'Enjoy your breakfast and stay in bed until it's warm enough to get up.'

'Has my uncle arisen yet?' Lucy asked.

'It's eight o'clock, Miss. The master always rises by seven every day. He has to be at court again today. Six men were caught by the revenue men and are to be sentenced today. I reckon they'll swing on yon gibbet before the weeks out.'

Lucy frowned. 'It seems a very drastic punishment for smuggling!'

'It is, Miss.' Molly agreed. 'Especially when those who dole out the punishment have never known what it is to be so hungry you think your insides are shrivelling. You do anything to get money for a meal!'

'I can understand what drives people to smuggle contraband,' she agreed.

Lucy thought Folly Cove would be a quiet place, but she was learning it was a hotbed of smuggling and her own uncle could be involved!

With Tobias away in Falcombe, Lucy decided, as it appeared to be a fine morning she would explore the gardens. It was a sunny day, but very cold. The gravel drive made a sweeping arch through the grounds which were much more extensive than she imagined. Molly had hot chocolate waiting for her when she went to the kitchen. They both sat by the fire sipping the delicious drink made with creamy milk.

Lucy was just about to comment on the fact Elvira was late returning when the housekeeper strode in.

'Good morning, Mrs Samuel.' Lucy greeted her pleasantly.

'You have a visitor in the parlour. It's Mr Trenarren and I thought you should try to calm him down as he appears to be in an angry mood.'

'What am I expected to do, Mrs Samuel? I know nothing of my uncle's affairs.'

Elvira sent her a disdainful look. 'Surely a young lady like yourself knows how to entertain a gentleman?'

'If what you say is correct and he is in an angry frame of mind, I doubt he is amiable to what I have to say,' she replied in a sharp tone. 'Also, since when do I take orders from you!'

'Well I'm sure I didn't mean to order you!' she replied in a flustered manner. It was obvious she had not expected Lucy to reprimand her.

Lucy left the kitchen feeling a tinge of satisfaction at her first small victory over the odious woman.

When she entered the parlour, Marcus Trenarren was standing near the fire, staring pensively into the flames, which today were burning brightly. He turned and something for a brief moment sparked in his deep blue eyes at the sight of her.

'Good day, Miss Armitage. I hope you are settling in your new home?' He smiled, but Lucy sensed he was keeping himself in check and underneath his temper was simmering.

'Yes, I am, Mr Trenarren thank you. My uncle has gone into Falcombe and I do not know when he is expected back.'

'So it is a case of the bird has flown.' His fine lips tightened.

'I'm certain he would have been here if it was possible. He has gone to court to deal out sentences, I believe,' she said in a cold tone.

He moved towards her. 'I would hazard a guess that you know very little of your uncle's character or his dealings, Miss Armitage, am I correct?' He fixed her with a steely gaze.

'That is true. My parents broke

contact with Tobias several years ago.'

'You were never told the reason, not even when you reached adulthood?'

'Tobias did not want my mother to move so far away from Cornwall to live in Yorkshire, or so my father informed me.'

'Come here, please, Miss Armitage and sit down.' Marcus poured wine into two glasses and handed one to her. He waited until she had seated herself on the settle before bringing one of the dining chairs close to the fire opposite her.

'I think you should know what kind of a man your uncle is.' He paused. 'I realise this will come as a shock, but Tobias has gambled away all he possesses.'

Lucy had held suspicions regarding her uncle's financial matters, judging by the general run down state of the house, but she still felt a sense of shock to be told outright and in such a forthright manner by this stranger.

'But how and who does he owe

everything to?' she asked in a stunned whisper.

Marcus' lips twisted in a wry expression. 'To the man who sits before you! He is deeply in debt to the tune of several hundred pounds and the only way he can extract himself from such misfortune is to sign this house over to me. Not only that, I demand it of him!'

4

The implications of Marcus Trenarren's startling revelations were just beginning to sink in. She rose to her feet. 'You cannot take someone's property and land on the turn of a card or whatever silly game you were playing!'

'The silly game you refer to was Tobias' idea. He had been losing all evening. I was not at the gaming table, only observing, but he dragged me into it deliberately by making a derogatory remark regarding my father and saying I had not the guts to take him on.

'I don't know if you are aware my father and your uncle were enemies. It was to do with Penelope, she was my elder sister. My father did not want her to marry Tobias, but we won't go into that now. To get back to Tobias' slur on my family, I could not allow that to go unchallenged by a man who has lost all sense of responsibility and decency.'

'And what of me?' She stared into his eyes, eyes that were hard and cold, devoid of compassion or so it seemed to her. 'Where do I come in your scheme of things?'

'I must admit your arrival was a surprise. Tobias should not have allowed you to journey all this way when he knew his house and possessions were forfeit.'

'I have no other home! My uncle felt responsible for me as I do not receive my inheritance until I attain my twenty-first year. I am his only relative and heir!'

Marcus laughed. 'Heir to what? Tobias has nothing left to leave to you!'

'You are a cruel, unfeeling man!' she denounced, two high spots of colour in her cheeks.

'Sit down, Miss Armitage.' He rose to his feet and moving to her, he placed his hands on her shoulders and gently pushed her down on to the settle.

'My character is not in question at

this present time. The important thing is, what do I do with you?'

'You need not do anything with me! I am not an appendage that goes with the house!'

'I beg to differ, Miss Armitage.' Marcus smiled grimly. 'When I own this house, you will be as much my responsibility as you were your uncle's.' He suddenly looked concerned. 'Are you all right? You've gone very pale!'

He moved to the table on which was a decanter of brandy. Pouring a good measure into a glass, he brought it to her and ordered her to drink it.

The strong liquid warmed and burned her throat and made her cough. 'I'm sorry all this has happened, especially since you have just arrived here.' His tone was softer, full of sympathy. 'But honour must be upheld. Tobias and I played a fair game and he lost. He must now face the conse-quences. You are the innocent one in all this. I will not see you homeless. You may stay here or at Craghill Hall, my family home, but your uncle will have to shift for himself.' His tone became hard again.

'Everything has happened so quickly.' She blinked away the tears threatening to spill down her cheeks. 'Yesterday I am told by my uncle this house will be left to me after his death. Today I learn it has all been taken away on the turn of a card!'

Marcus bent down to her and took her hands in his cool ones. A feeling raced through her which she could not ignore, then Tobias' warning entered her head.

Marcus has a bad reputation with the ladies. Steer well clear of him.

'Do you feel better now?' he asked gently.

'Yes, thank you. How soon do you intend to be master here?'

'That depends on your uncle. If he pays what he owes me, then the house remains his, and your inheritance is safe.'

'I am not dependent on this house

for my livelihood!' she said crossly. 'In one year's time I will be a fully independent woman!'

'I'm sure you will be,' he murmured, his gaze sweeping like a caress over her pink cheeks and indignant features.

'I will wait no longer for your uncle.' He got up to leave. 'Tell him I have consulted my lawyers and he will be hearing from them if he does not intend to settle this as he promised. I bid you farewell, Miss Armitage.'

Lucy paced the parlour for a long time after Marcus had gone. To learn that her mother's brother was a serious gambler was a shock in itself, but to gamble all his assets was deeply disturbing.

Dare she confront Tobias? How could she when he had been kind enough to invite her to High Ridge when she had been facing homelessness. With no employment she would have been destitute. But why had he brought her here when he knew there was a chance he could lose everything? Was he intending to pay Marcus Trenarren what he owed him?

And what of Marcus himself? What did she know of him? Would he keep his promise to allow her to remain at High Ridge? Did he have a wife and would she be agreeable to the arrangement? She was so immersed in her thoughts she did not hear the door open.

Tobias watched for several seconds as she paced up and down, her pale features creased in concentration.

'Whatever is the matter, niece?' He moved towards her and clasped her hands in his ice cold ones. 'You look as though the weight of the whole world is on your shoulders!'

'Marcus Trenarren has been here!' She related what Marcus had said.

His features darkened. 'That man is nothing but a plague on me and his father before him!' His eyes narrowed suspiciously. 'Why do you look so concerned? What else did he say?'

'It is not a matter of what Marcus Trenarren said, rather the fact of what you haven't told me what is causing me this distress!' She realised now was the time for speaking out. 'Tell me truthfully, what was the cause of the quarrel between you and my father? Would it be because he disapproved of your custom of frequenting the gaming tables?'

'Marcus Trenarren had no right discussing my private affairs with you! It is entirely a matter between him and myself!' Tobias said, seething with suppressed rage.

'If it affects me then of course he had a right! Why did you invite me here, knowing you could lose this house?'

'I will not lose the house!' he snapped. 'Whatever Marcus Trenarren told you, do you think I would risk losing High Ridge which has belonged to the Penmaricks for generations? He will be paid shortly. I will soon have the means to replace all I have lost and put this house to rights. I'm sure you would like some new pretty gowns, wouldn't you, my dear?'

Lucy stared at him, wondering where the money was forthcoming from to pay his debts. 'You still have not answered my question about the reason for the quarrel between yourself and my father,' Lucy persisted.

'Well, as it appears I can no longer keep it a secret,' he said irritably. 'Yes, it was regarding my gambling. Your father was always a prude and a killjoy. There's nothing wrong in a little pleasure now and again.'

'A little pleasure!' Lucy exclaimed incredulously. 'You are on the verge of losing all you possess!'

'That's over-dramatising it a little. Marcus incensed me with his arrogance and I goaded him into the winner takes all game. He has always hated me since I married his sister, Penelope.'

'But how will you pay what you owe?' she asked.

Tobias smiled. 'I have some money owed to me, don't worry. Now we will forget Marcus Trenarren's threats and have our luncheon.'

Over the meal, Tobias appeared to be in a happier frame of mind. He seemed so certain he could pay the debt he owed Marcus. Lucy sincerely hoped he was not merely prevaricating to delay the inevitable.

The following week passed uneventfully. Marcus Trenarren did not return to High Ridge issuing threats, causing Lucy to hope that Tobias had indeed settled the debt. There was no opportunity to walk out or visit Falcombe for several days. The weather closed in, bringing driving rain and cold, biting winds. At high tide the sea pounded ferociously at the interior of the caves, making an eerie rumbling noise Lucy found difficult to ignore.

One day she entered her bedroom to find dozens of boxes of all shapes and sizes on the bed. Opening them she found Tobias had been as good as his word. The clothing spilling from the boxes was of the finest quality. There were several day dresses, fine woollen and soft velvet and smooth satin ones.

The three ballgowns in delicate floating muslin were in pale shades of blue and lilac and a pure white one with embroidery running through the material which shimmered like gold. Lucy gaped in awe, she had never seen such clothing.

Besides the nightdresses and underwear, there were half a dozen pairs of shoes and bonnets to match the high-waisted coats. There was a muff of the softest fur and she held her face to it, unable to believe her uncle would spend such an amount on her and how had he guessed her size?

Holding up another outfit, she realised it was for riding. Lucy had not ridden a horse since she was thirteen. After her father died, luxuries such as horse riding were out of the question.

She intended to thank Tobias for his generosity during the evening meal that night, but Elvira informed her he had business to attend to and would not return to the house until late so Lucy ate a solitary-meal.

After the meal Lucy felt restless. She had been cooped up in the house for days because of the inclement weather and it was too early to retire. She decided to walk around the grounds and take a breath of air. She chose a coat in a light grey heavy brocade fabric to wear over her dress. Elvira had announced earlier that as the master wasn't expected back until late, she would retire for the night. She had left Tobias his supper in the parlour.

Lucy was pleased the housekeeper would not be around to criticise her decision to have a walk. Elvira made a habit of disapproving of almost everything she did. From what she ate to the clothes she wore, but not any more. Lucy was not a vain person, but she knew these clothes brought out the best of her features.

She let herself out of the rear door. The air was crisp and fresh and she breathed in deeply the salt tainted breeze from the sea. Lucy felt she was beginning to settle at High Ridge and would be loathe to leave the sea and have to return to city life. Eventually it would have to end when she received her inheritance. But why should it? This place was to be hers when Tobias died. It was her home now, the only one she had. She could make her life here permanent and perhaps one day marry?

The moment the thought of marriage entered her head so did Marcus Trenarren. Why should she think of that egotistical arrogant popinjay? Tobias had warned her against him, but she now knew her uncle had reason to dislike him. Foolish girl! She chided herself.

The night was turning colder as it was still only February. She walked by the numerous dark unlit windows of the house and was about to turn in the direction of the Folly steps when a flash of light out at sea caught her eye. She watched for several minutes until it began to move away and she could see it no longer. The splash of oars, close to the shore warned her a boat was coming in. Was it Jack Malvern and his cronies bringing cargo in to hide in the cave while the tide was out?

Should she tell Tobias she had suspicions they were hiding contraband in the cave under the house? But she couldn't do that when only the other day she had glanced out of a window and seen in the distance a corpse swinging from the gibbet.

Lucy began to retrace her steps to the rear door when it suddenly opened and a yellow light spilled out on to the paved terrace. It was Elvira carrying a lantern. Lucy flattened herself against the side of the house. Elvira hurried towards the Folly steps and disappeared down them.

Where was she going? Had she too seen the light and was going to investigate? But she was a local and knew it was wiser to turn your face away and pretend not to have seen anything suspicious.

Lucy could not follow Elvira down those steps even if she wanted to, without a lantern. The steps were precarious enough in daylight. She walked to the top of the steps. Now she could hear voices on the beach and the sound of the boat being dragged towards the cave.

The sharp sound of pistol fire startled her and she spun round quickly. As she did so, loose gravel broke away under her feet and showered down the steps.

Lucy panicked. If those men below thought someone was spying on them, they would stop at nothing to protect themselves! Her fears were justified when shots were fired again from below, but this time aimed in her direction.

She turned and fled towards the house, then stumbled and almost fell. It was the arms, reaching from behind which saved her. She opened her mouth to scream, but a hand was too quick and closed over it to stifle her call for help.

'If you promise to keep quiet, I will

remove my hand. Scream and we both could be in trouble,' he whispered. 'The Riding Officer and dragoons are combing the beach and cliffs at this very moment. I am going to take my hand away. You will not make a sound?'

She shook her head and Marcus removed his hand but still maintained his hold around her waist. 'Why are you here? What . . . '

'Not now. Come, we mustn't be seen.' He took her arm in a forceful grip and propelled her towards the house. Once inside he began to slide the bolt into place.

'You can't lock the door. Elvira is out there. She didn't see me, but I watched her go down the steps to the cove.'

'Elvira Samuel. I suspected she would be involved,' he mused half to himself.

'I am more interested at this moment why you are prowling around here, Mr Trenarren.' She shrugged off his arm which still held on to her.

'Are you, Miss Armitage? Well,

perhaps I'm not prepared to give you an explanation right now.' His tone was mocking.

She could not see his features in the dark passageway, but there was a hint of menace mixed with the mockery in his voice. A wave of fear swept through her. He had not wanted the King's men to see them. Was he one of the smugglers?

They both jumped visibly when there was a commotion outside and heavy pounding on the door. 'Open up in there! Custom Officers on the King's business!' a commanding voice rang out.

'Go upstairs and hide where you can!' Lucy urged. 'I'll try and delay them from searching!'

'Don't answer the door yet and take off your outdoor things!' he whispered.

Lucy quickly did as he directed. She went to the kitchen and collected a candlestick before returning to open the door. She was terrified, but if she could prevent it, she would not let them capture Marcus. There were certain questions she wanted answering first!

5

Lucy walked slowly to the outer door. She drew back the bolt and tried to steady the trembling in her hand which held the candlestick. Taking a deep breath she opened the door.

The Riding Officer was a tall burly man with broad shoulders who filled the door frame. Lucy had to tilt her head back to look at him. There was a determined expression in his steely stare.

'I beg your pardon, Madam, for disturbing you at this late hour. My name is Matthew Cornby of the Custom House, Riding Officer for this area. I am attempting to apprehend certain people who are carrying out smuggling activities. One of them came into these grounds but a few minutes ago. I'm sure you will have heard the shots? Have you seen anyone near the house?'

'Certainly not, sir. I was about to retire to bed,' she said, putting a hand to her mouth to stifle a pretend yawn.

'Could we search the house to ascertain no-one has entered by an unlocked window or door?'

'I can assure you, sir, all the windows and doors are securely locked by Mrs Samuel, the housekeeper. I cannot give you permission to enter my uncle's house when he is not here. As you may be aware he is the local magistrate and will take a dim view of your intrusion into his home.'

Matthew Cornby appeared undecided. 'Very well, Madam. If you do see anything suspicious it is your duty to report it to the Revenue officers.'

'I will, sir. Now will you please allow me to go to my bed? I am quite chilly standing here.'

'I apologise, Madam and I will bid you a goodnight.'

He touched his hat and turned, giving orders to his men to continue to search the grounds. Lucy closed the door and slid the bolt into place. Then she remembered Elvira. She would just have to wait until Marcus had safely left the house.

Lucy was on her way to the upper floor when she heard Marcus calling her. She ran back down and found him in the formal dining-room which Tobias no longer used. The room had glass doors, leading out to the rose garden.

Lucy peered out to make certain the Revenue men were not still searching the grounds. All was still and silent, but she drew the heavy brocade curtains closed which, apart from her own room, was the only one with such luxury. She lit the candelabra and turned to look at Marcus. The flickering pale light revealed the uncertainty in her eyes.

'Tobias may return at any minute and I must go and unlock the back door for Elvira. You cannot stay long.'

'I don't intend to,' he drawled, half leaning on the table, one foot placed on a chair.

'Unless you would like to offer me hospitality.'

'I think not!' she exclaimed indignantly. 'Would you explain what you were doing out there?'

'I could ask you the same. You could have been killed!'

'I live here! I have a right to walk around the grounds. Why didn't you want the Revenue men to see you? Are you involved in something unlawful?'

'I have been waiting for a ship to arrive from France for several days now. Unfortunately the cargo I was expecting wasn't on it.'

'So you are a smuggler!' she gasped.

'I have not said so. You can jump to any conclusions you wish, Miss Armitage.'

'What else am I to think,' she replied.

'You are perfectly free to think what you like. I am not at liberty to say what my business is. You made enough noise out there to send the whole county after you. If it had been anyone but me that got to you first, you would have had a lot of explaining to do and some of these people can get rough!' he stated grimly.

'You are saying I should thank you then?' Her tone was sarcastic.

'That will do for a start,' he said softly mocking. He moved away from the table and joined her near the window.

'Has Tobias paid his debt to you?' she asked, trying to ignore the effects his nearness was having on her.

'Yes, he has. I have my suspicions however as to how he obtained such a large amount. Are you disappointed I won't be master here?' The mockery was evident in his tone.

'Why should I be disappointed, Mr Trenarren? You are a stranger to me. My family have owned this house for generations. I want it to stay in the family.'

'When you inherit the house and marry, it will no longer belong to the Penmaricks, will it?' His keen gaze searched her features.

'I may never marry,' she answered.

'If that is so who inherits High Ridge?' he taunted.

He put into words something she had not considered. The fact of her being an heiress was something new and she had not weighed up the possibilities. It made her feel beholden to marry and the thought was strangely depressing. She was about to change the subject and ask him what his remark meant regarding his suspicions of her uncle when there was the sound of the main door opening.

'You must go! That will be Tobias returning!'

'Pity, I was enjoying our conversation.' Marcus mocked.

Lucy drew aside the curtain after blowing out the candles. She quietly turned the window key.

'One word of warning, Miss Armitage.' Marcus whispered, catching hold of her arm. 'Don't go wandering around after dark. There are dangerous activities in this area, besides the fact there are also dangers from the French, now Bonaparte is expected to return to power again. There are spies all over and invasion is a real threat! Until our next meeting, I wish you goodnight.'

He took her hand and held it to his lips. His kiss on her skin was cool and a shiver went through her. Then he was gone into the darkness.

Lucy quietly closed the window and locked it. She went into the hall and came face to face with Tobias.

'Oh, Tobias you startled me!' she said, wondering if he had heard her speaking to Marcus.

'Why are you up so late, niece?' His dark eyes shifted suspiciously over her features.

'I've been checking the windows and doors Tobias, to make certain they are secure. I was on my way to my room to retire for the night when the soldiers arrived with a Riding Officer. They were apparently pursuing someone who was acting suspiciously on the beach. They believed he had fled into the grounds.'

'A Riding Officer, here you say? Have you seen anyone near the house?' Tobias searched her features keenly.

'No, I was just afraid there may have been a door or window left unlocked.'

'Did they enquire as to my whereabouts?' he asked.

'No and I would not have been able to enlighten them, would I?'

'Do not look so concerned, my dear. This is a perfectly respectable household and we do not harbour criminals of any kind. Has Elvira retired for the night?'

'Yes, I believe so, Tobias.'

'Good, now you run along to your bed. I'll see you in the morning. I have a free day and we will ride into Falcombe. I have arranged with Watson, the coachman to stop and pick us up at ten. I have a surprise for you.'

'I shall look forward to that, Tobias, but I have already had a lovely surprise today when I discovered all those clothes in my room, for which I thank you. I really did not expect to own such beautiful clothes.'

Tobias gave one of his rare smiles. 'Nonsense, you deserve them. I'm sure before long some young buck will be asking for your hand.'

Lucy bade him good night and was about to climb the stairs when she remembered she had left the rear door locked. Elvira was still out.

'May I heat some milk to take up to my room, Tobias?'

'Certainly, my dear. Good night.' He walked away to the parlour, leaving Lucy to believe she was not the only one looking concerned. When he'd heard the Revenue men had been searching the grounds an expression almost of fear had crossed his features.

Lucy went to unlock the outer door before she heated her milk. Where was Elvira? Had Matthew Cornby and his soldiers caught her?

Taking her drink up to her room, Lucy undressed and got into bed. Her mind was racing through the events of the evening and she found herself unable to sleep.

Lucy awoke and turned over. As she did so the icy cold air invaded the bed; shivering she pulled the covers around her head. Elvira had not appeared yet to wake her.

She must have dozed again as the next thing she knew Elvira was standing over her, shaking her shoulders. Her face appeared pale and gaunt in the early morning light and she looked as if she'd had very little sleep herself.

'Miss Armitage, wake up! The master has told me to make sure you are ready to catch the ten o'clock coach to Falcombe.'

Lucy glanced to the mantel clock. It was past nine. She had not meant to lie in so late. Being unable to sleep during the night it was inevitable she would doze off when it was time to get up. She accepted the breakfast tray and hurriedly ate the porridge and scrambled eggs.

After she had eaten, Lucy quickly chose something to wear. Never in her life had she so many clothes. She finally plumped for a fine woollen dress in lilac with a navy coat and hat to match with a jaunty lilac feather.

Tobias was waiting in the parlour when she entered. 'You look so much like your mother when she was your age,' he remarked, a brief glimpse of emotion in his eyes. 'Come, if you are ready. Watson is waiting with the coach.'

'Where are we going?' Lucy ventured to ask as they stepped outside the front entrance.

'You will see when we reach Falcombe,' he replied enigmatically.

He helped her into the coach and Watson set the horses in motion. They travelled along the wide gravel drive and through the imposing iron gates. Tobias withdrew into himself and seemed to be preoccupied with his thoughts.

Before long the coach was making its way through the cobbled streets of Falcombe. It was larger than Lucy imagined. Some of the streets near the harbour were narrow with white-washed cottages, but there were also wider thoroughfares with shops selling a wide variety of goods, even a milliner and dress shop. Lucy's interest was held until Tobias announced they had reached their destination.

She glanced out and saw they had halted at a livery stable. Tobias helped her out and the coach moved off.

'Come this way, my dear.'

Intrigued she followed him into the yard. A stable boy was at that moment leading a magnificent pair of white horses into the centre of the yard. He began to harness them to an elegant carriage with gleaming brass work.

'What do you think of your surprise, niece?' Tobias asked, a hint of pride in his voice. 'Are they not magnificent?'

Lucy could only stare at him. 'Do you mean they are ours?'

'Ours, yours, whenever you wish to use them. And this is for you alone to ride.'

Lucy turned to look as a beautiful

chestnut mare was led towards her. The creature appeared to be of a gentle nature with soft doe eyes. There was a white strip down its nose and she knew immediately what name she would give it.

'I shall call her Blaze. Thank you so much, Tobias. I have not ridden for seven years and I thought I would never own a horse again.' A frown lined her brow. 'Surely all this must cost a huge amount of money?'

'That is not for you to worry about, my dear. I can afford it now. I have already employed a groom and a stable boy to get the old stable at High Ridge ready and I am employing other help in the house to relieve Elvira.' A gleam of pride entered his eyes. 'High Ridge will be brought back to its former glory. For too long now it has been neglected.'

'You suddenly have an inordinate sum of money to spend, Penmarick! I would be interested to know where it was all acquired from?'

They both spun round at the steely,

sarcastic tones. Marcus Trenarren had just entered the yard, leading his black stallion which was limping.

'I'm sure you would, Trenarren, but that is information you will never learn, mind your own business and leave me to mine. Come, my dear.' Tobias took Lucy's arm.

Marcus' gaze swept over Lucy with something like disdain in their depths. 'Good morning, Miss Armitage. I see you are enjoying the fruits of your uncle's dubious wealth!'

He raised his hat to her in polite mockery. Lucy was embarrassed by his forthright sarcasm. She murmured a greeting and followed Tobias to the carriage.

6

The wind stung Lucy's cheeks as she raced Blaze across open country near High Ridge. In the last few days horse and rider had quickly formed a bond. Sometimes, when the tide was out they would take their exercise along the beach, close to the water. It was possible to ride all the way to Falcombe and Lucy thrilled to the exhilaration of the wind catching at her loosened hair.

At times she would dismount and sit on a rock, gazing out to sea, contemplating how her life had changed in the short month she had lived at High Ridge. The old house had seemed so sparse and bleak she never thought she would settle, but now there was a transformation taking place. New furniture and curtains were arriving by the week and Tobias had employed new servants who came to the house daily to clean.

Invitations began to arrive from the local gentry, who having heard of Tobias Penmarick's good fortune appeared anxious to meet his pretty niece. Lucy's stomach twisted into knots at the thought of being paraded around the numerous drawing rooms of Falcombe and surrounding area. Tobias seemed keen for her to meet every eligible bachelor and was at a loss to understand her reluctance to mix in social circles.

She turned Blaze's head and set off for home. She thought of High Ridge as home now. Her life in Yorkshire was in the past and now she was to inherit the house there was no reason to return to her native county.

The crossroads gibbet stood stark on the horizon. She averted her eyes from the corpse swinging there as she rode past. It was hard to contemplate her own uncle was responsible for the man's death.

When she arrived at the house, Lucy left Blaze in the care of the new stable boy. She entered the house through the door which led by the kitchen. She glanced in to see Molly sitting at the table in a distressed state. Lizzie, the new kitchen maid was trying to comfort her.

Lucy went in and taking a kerchief from the pocket of her riding habit she handed it to Molly. 'Whatever is the matter, Molly?' she asked.

'Oh, Miss Armitage, the master has said he no longer wishes me to work here, after all these years!'

Lucy instructed Lizzie to heat up the kettle and make some tea. 'But why? You are a decent, honest worker,' she asked, turning back to Molly.

Molly wiped her tears with the kerchief. 'Something even more dreadful's happened! The Riding Officer caught my nephew and some other men coming in with booty a few days ago. The master is going to have them stand trial in a few days time and says he can't be seen to have relatives of criminals working for him!'

'But that is not your fault, Molly. I

shall speak to him on your behalf.'

'I doubt it will do any good, Miss. Ben, my nephew is only a young lad. It was his first time and he only did it to get a bit o' pay until he could go crabbing again. The master won't do anything bad to him, will he? He's my sister's lad and now she has no husband she relies on Ben to keep soul and body together. I don't know what they are going to do to survive?'

'I'll do my best to help her, Molly. I'll give your sister provisions until we see what the outcome is. What about you and your husband? How will you manage?'

'I don't know, Miss Armitage. I'm not taking anything from Tobias Penmarick, apart from what he owes me in wages.'

'I will help you also, Molly. Tobias gives me a monthly allowance. He will know nothing about it.'

'God bless you, Miss. If it's at all possible, when we get over this we'll pay back every penny.'

'Don't worry about that now, Molly.' Lucy tried to reassure her. 'Give me your address and we will go tomorrow to see your sister. I will pick you up from your home.'

It was later, over supper that Lucy clashed with Tobias over his dismissal of Molly. 'How can I keep control over these people who have no regard for the law if I'm still employing them?' he snapped.

'Molly has no other means of support. Her husband is not a well man and now her sister's son is one of those about to stand trial for smuggling, the whole family will be destitute!'

Tobias' expression was cold. 'You know nothing of these things, niece. I suggest you concentrate on your own affairs and leave me to mine! If the men are found guilty they will hang as a warning to others, including the boy!'

'If people are starving they will risk barbaric punishment to obtain food!' Lucy exclaimed.

Tobias wiped his mouth on a napkin

and rose to his feet. 'I will not discuss the matter further, niece. If you wish to remain in my house I advise you to keep your thoughts to yourself! Now, I have business to attend to. I am taking the carriage into Falcombe.'

When Tobias had gone, Lucy let out a great sigh. Her uncle was intransigent. It was apparent all he cared about was doing his duty as a magistrate and not one jot for the people he condemned and their families. Some time later she heard the carriage head down the drive. Where was he going at this late hour? Surely he was still not gambling?

The next day, Lucy arose determined to ignore Tobias' threat. She would not stand idly by while innocent people suffered the consequence of the harsh laws regarding smuggling, meted out by her uncle. Thankfully Tobias had gone out early and not taken the coach.

Lucy had chosen to wear one of her old plain dresses over which she wore a thick black cloak and grey linen bonnet. She was going to offer her help, not flaunt her newly-found wealth and lose the trust she wished to build with Molly's sister.

'May I enquire where you are going, Miss Armitage, in the event your uncle returns early'

Elvira's inquisitive tone startled Lucy as she made her way across the hall to set off on her errand. She turned to face the housekeeper's hard stare, taking in the large basket on Lucy's arm.

'I am going into Falcombe, Mrs Samuel, to look at the shops. Anything else you would like to know?'

'The master may not approve of you using the carriage so frequently.'

'My uncle bought the coach and horses specifically for both our use. I am going to speak plainly, Mrs Samuel. You may not like my presence in this house, but I'm here and here to stay. High Ridge will be mine one day!'

Elvira paled. It was obvious she believed Lucy would return to Yorkshire one day when her inheritance was due to be released.

'Has the master given you reason to believe so?' she asked, her eyes dark with an expression of shock.

'Of course he has. Who else would he leave it to?' Lucy replied in stern tone.

For once Elvira was lost for words. Lucy walked away, leaving her to mull over the revelation.

The coach took Lucy into Falcombe, where she purchased, from her monthly allowance, the provisions which she thought would be most needed — flour, eggs, tea, a side of ham, potatoes and vegetables.

The coach halted outside Molly's cottage to pick her up then continued down the cobbled street, leading to the harbour where her sister, Joan lived.

'Can we stop the coach here, Miss Lucy? I'd rather we go the rest of the way on foot. I don't know what my sister's reaction will be if she sees this grand coach. Tobias Penmarick is hated in these parts now.'

Lucy understood. These fishing people were poor, but proud and they might take offence at having their poverty so starkly accentuated. She called to the coachman to halt and they stepped out. Lucy gave instructions to the coachman to return to High Ridge. She intended to walk back along the beach,

Eventually they reached her sister's immaculate white washed cottage. The interior of the cottage was just as spick and span. Joan was younger looking than Molly and she drew herself up proudly as Molly introduced her.

'I'll not beat about the bush, Miss Armitage. If it wasn't for my sister here I wouldn't have let you step foot over that threshold, but beggars can't be choosers. Since my Ben's been incarcerated by your uncle there's not a scrap of food coming into this house. I've been relying on my sister for food.'

'I do not agree with the harsh punishments my uncle gives out, but neither do I condone smuggling either, Mrs Lock. All I want to do, within my power, is to help until we know what the outcome will be for Ben and those other men.'

Joan's features crumpled and the tears began to flow down her face. Molly motioned to Lucy to sit on the paddled window seat.

'Miss Armitage has brought you some provisions, Joan, to tide you over.' Molly held her sister until the sobbing had subsided.

Lucy emptied the contents of the basket on the table and went to sit down.

'Ben's not a bad boy, he's only fourteen and intended to do one job only, just to help us out until he can go back to fishing,' Joan explained. 'Your uncle just wants to make an example out of him cos he's so young.'

'Yes, I understand.' Lucy murmured sympathetically. 'I have spoken with my uncle and I will try all I can to help Ben.'

They all turned as the door swung open and a man and woman walked in. it was Kate from the Tor Head Inn and

Jack Malvern. A closed, hostile expression crossed his features when he saw Lucy.

'What's she doing here? We don't want the likes of her sort gloating over us!' He strode over to Lucy and grasped her arm, pulling her to her feet.

'Jack, leave her alone!' Joan spoke up. 'She's coming to help me and Molly. Look at the food she's brought us!'

Jack brought his face close to Lucy's. 'Do you think a bit of food can make up for what that double crossing uncle of yours is doing!'

'I'm not responsible for what Tobias does.' Lucy answered, feeling afraid.

Kate moved towards Jack and dragged him away from Lucy. 'She's right. Don't blame her, Jack. I reckon she doesn't know the half of what that precious uncle of hers gets up to.'

'What do you mean?' Lucy asked.

Jack shrugged off Kate's hand on his arm. 'Apart from his weakness for cheating at the gaming tables your law abiding upright relative is head of one of the biggest smuggling gangs in the county! Trouble is now the Revenue men are plaguing the area, he's turned traitor to those who have made him rich! Afraid his neck might feel the rope next. But who's going to believe the likes of me? It's his word against ours.'

Lucy stared at him. Even though she suspected Tobias, to be actually confronted with the fact her uncle was head of a smuggling ring was too much to take in!

'I don't believe you! You want revenge for the capture of Ben and the others!' she exclaimed.

'Well, my fine lady, where do you think your uncle's sudden wealth has come from?' Jack sneered. 'Not just from cheating at the gaming table. A pretty little ship from France frequents these shores, laden with spirits, tobacco and other trinkets. Where do you think all that booty might be hidden, eh?'

'In the cave under High Ridge!' she whispered. Her eyes were wide with horror as she contemplated what it all could mean if it came to light.

'You must remove the stuff as quickly as possible!' she urged. 'Surely you have other hiding places?'

Jack laughed, but there was no merriment in the sound. 'We did have, but it was discovered when Ben and the others were caught. It can't stay in that cave. It's on a wide ledge, but there's a chance the sea could reach it and ruin the whole lot. Now, what I propose is we move it. Help us and there might be a spot of brandy and some lace for you.'

'I wouldn't touch it!' Lucy replied with contempt.

'Tobias knows the booty is in that cave, but to shut him up I'm going to move it to the cellars under the house. Mr High and Mighty magistrate can't deny involvement when it's under his own roof, can he? You can help Ma shift the stuff. She can't do it on her own. Two of you can soon get it moved.'

'I will not get involved!'

Jack grinned. 'You already are, now

go home and have a word with Ma. Run to your uncle with tales and I can't be responsible for what might happen!'

'Please don't involve her in your dirty trade, Jack,' Molly begged him. 'She promised to help us with food.'

'And so she should! The Penmaricks owe us!' Jack spat into the fire.

'I'd better go.' Lucy picked up the basket and hurried to the door.

'I'll see you out.' Kate said, following her outside. 'Miss Armitage, Lucy. I appreciate what you're doing for my mother and Aunt Molly.'

'Joan is your mother?' Lucy asked.

'Yes, Ben is my young brother, my only brother and if anything happens to him it will kill our mother!'

'I understand, Kate, but I can't move that contraband into the cellars of High Ridge and incriminate my own uncle! You heard what Jack said if Tobias was found out.'

Kate stared at her, tears forming in her eyes. 'If you don't my brother will hang!'

Lucy realised she was in an impossible dilemma! It was clear Kate was hoping Tobias would be blackmailed into releasing Ben when he realised the smuggled goods were on his property.

Lucy suddenly made up her mind. She couldn't let a young boy like Ben face the prospect of execution when he had become involved in smuggling as a means of making a living to support his mother. Tobias would not dare condemn those men while contraband was on his own property. Jack Malvern would ensure the Revenue men were told of that!

'Very well, I'll move the contraband into the cellars, but you must help me. I don't want to ask Elvira, even though I suspected all along she was involved in the trade.'

'The less that old witch knows, the better,' Kate scoffed. 'Can you get the key to the cellar?'

'It's Elvira's half-day tomorrow. I will be in charge of the servants so she will hand the keys to me.'

'I'll be there tomorrow afternoon then. I've finished at the Tor Head, Jack didn't like me working there.'

At that moment, Jack came striding out of the cottage. 'What are you two talking about?' His tone was menacing.

It was then Lucy saw fear in Kate's eyes. She visibly flinched when he grasped her arm none too gently and began to drag her away. 'Don't forget. I'll be making sure you move that stuff!' he threatened.

Lucy walked quickly away without answering. She suddenly became aware of a horse and rider almost upon her. Lucy glanced up, startled to see Marcus Trenarren staring down at her.

'I saw you talking to Jack Malvern and it appeared he was threatening you, am I correct?'

'I would appreciate it if you mind your own business, Mr Trenarren and allow me to go on my way!'

In that moment she had a sudden longing to tell him everything, but realised she did not really know him. Was he law abiding or like Tobias, using the cover of respectability to hide his lawless dealings? Was anyone what they appeared to be in this place?

7

'Why should you concern yourself about me, Mr Trenarren? I am perfectly capable of looking after myself!'

'I very much doubt that when the likes of Jack Malvern threatens you!'

Lucy sensed she could not conceal the reason from him and in a curious way she didn't want to. She felt she needed someone to confide in, but she could not tell him about the contraband in the cave. She still did not know where his loyalties lay.

'If you must know, I was visiting Mrs Lock, sister of Molly who works for my uncle, did work for him. He dismissed her yesterday on the pretext he could not employ anyone whose relatives were involved in smuggling. Molly has worked for Tobias for years!'

'He certainly knows how to be popular and he's not exactly a saint himself,' he remarked with sarcasm in his tone.

Lucy glanced up at him. Did he know Tobias was the leader of a smuggling gang? If he did his next words did not reveal it.

'He is still at the gaming tables after all that has happened! He has learnt nothing!' He shook his head in exasperation.

'Molly's nephew and some other men were caught with contraband.' Lucy explained. 'I've taken some food to Mrs Lock. She relies on Ben even though he's so young. He's never been mixed up in smuggling before and it was only one job until he can go back to fishing.'

'Yes, I have heard about the boy.' Marcus said, dismounting.

'Can you use your influence to help him, Mr Trenarren?' she asked. 'You are a well respected member of the neighbourhood.'

Marcus looked amused. 'Am I indeed? I think we can dispense with formalities now. You may call me

Marcus and I will call you Lucy, if I may?'

Lucy lowered her eyes. 'If you wish,' she said, colour flooding her cheeks. 'To get back to Mrs Lock's son, Ben. Will you please try to do all within your power to see he receives clemency?'

'Believe me, Lucy I will do my utmost to help him, if you will do something for me? Tell me what Jack Malvern has to do with you?'

She raised her head to look into eyes clouded with concern for her. 'I wish I could tell you, but I cannot.'

'Be assured I shall discover what is going on!' he stated in a determined tone. 'Where is your carriage?' He gazed along the street.

'I informed the coachman I would be walking home. I intend to go back along the beach.'

'Good. Spartan needs some more exercise. He also enjoys the beach.' He patted the stallion's neck. 'We shall ride part of the way and walk the rest.'

'Oh, I don't think . . . ' She had no

opportunity to protest further when Marcus scooped her up into his arms and lifted her on to Spartan's back. Her basket fell to the ground and Marcus picked it up and gave it to her to hold in front.

Once Marcus had hoisted himself into the saddle behind her and pressed her close to him, she realised she didn't want to protest. She was enjoying the feel of his strong arms around her waist.

Spartan trotted down to the cobbled harbour, where the stench of fish and seaweed made Lucy want to hold her kerchief over her nose, but the smell was soon forgotten when they came to the wide expanse of the bay with firm pale sand. The tide was well out and it was wonderful to briefly forget her problems and let Marcus take control of the sturdy beast, straining to have free rein and gallop along the edge of the waterline.

They had gone a good way before Marcus brought Spartan to a halt.

Away in the distance she could see High Ridge, perched majestically on the pinnacle of the cliff.

'Shall we walk now?' Marcus asked. 'I think Spartan deserves a rest, don't you?'

'I certainly do. That was so exhilarating!' she said, still feeling slightly breathless from the ride.

Marcus was about to help her down, but he paused a moment and took in her curls spilling from her bonnet and the pink glow of her cheeks. In that moment she appeared beautiful. He held her against him as he helped her slide from the saddle. She stiffened and he stood back, realising she might not welcome his advances.

Lucy knew when Marcus had held her close she had wanted more from him. The thought shocked her. She meant nothing to him, merely a distraction.

She turned away from his perceptive stare to give her time to recover from the gamut of emotions racing through her body. She would not be a source of amusement for him! To defuse the strained atmosphere she pointed out the grand house, set back from the cliffs, she had noticed from High Ridge.

'Who lives there?' she asked.

'Oh a very grand personage, but he's an utter cad and a rogue.' Marcus replied in a serious tone.

'If that is so and he is unattached I expect Tobias will invite him to High Ridge and parade me before him like a prize cow at a show!'

Marcus threw back his head and laughed loudly. 'I very much doubt that! That, my dear is Craghill Hall!'

She turned to stare at him. 'Craghill Hall?' She thought for a moment. 'But of course, you are teasing me! It is your home! You must think I am very silly.'

'Not at all. I love to watch the different emotions cross your face.' Suddenly the amusement in his eyes faded to be replaced with an expression which set her heart racing.

'Very soon I am holding an evening

soirée and I would very much like you to come,' he invited.

They began walking again and Lucy was glad her face was turned away. There was something in his tone which she hoped she was not misinterpreting. 'That would be impossible I fear. Tobias has warned me to stay away from you.'

'And you obey him implicitly?'

'Tobias gave me a home when I was near destitute after my mother died. He has bequeathed High Ridge to me. I owe him much.'

'Will you trust your future happiness to him?'

'I will not allow him to choose a suitor for me if that's what you mean?' she replied indignantly. 'As I have already stated, Tobias is anxious I find a suitable husband.'

'Are you anxious to find a husband?' He stared at her profile, watching her reaction closely.

'No, definitely not!' she exclaimed. 'Could we please change the subject!' She began to walk quickly in front. His low laugh infuriated her. Why did men always assume women wanted nothing more in life than to be tied in marriage?

Marcus caught her up. 'Forgive me if you believed I was using you for my own amusement. I realise behind that reserved exterior there is an intelligent, forceful, but also a warm, caring person. Give that loving heart to only someone who can return that love in equal measure.'

Lucy halted and met his gaze. There was no teasing now, but a look in the blue depths of his eyes which made her heart turn over. In that moment she knew with certainty she loved Marcus Trenarren.

Close to the cliff edge at High Ridge a figure was watching the pair in the distance. Tobias felt angry that Lucy was disobeying him and holding what appeared to be an intimate conversation with the son of his deceased enemy, but it was rage that boiled inside him at the audacity of Marcus Trenarren thinking he could court his niece. He was determined their acquaintance would go no further. If it did he would not be responsible for the consequences!

What was she thinking of, meeting Trenarren unchaperoned? Her reputation could be ruined! That reprobate was not going to take advantage of her. It was obvious he was only toying with her affections. The fury Tobias felt was threatening to erupt into murderous intent!

8

The plan to move the contraband into the cellar of the house began to go wrong when Tobias made his announcement the following morning.

Lucy was crossing the hall, intending to ask the head groom to saddle Blaze, when Tobias opened the parlour door and informed her he wished to discuss a certain matter.

Lucy entered and not for the first time since Tobias came upon good fortune, she was amazed at the transformation of the room. A thick carpet covered a large proportion of the floor now and the velvet dark red curtains gave the room a cosy feel. The fire blazed high in the hearth and there was the addition of two new couches. Lucy seated herself at Tobias' indication on one of them.

'We have been invited out this

evening, my dear at a soirée held by Lord Huntingdon of Ledley Manor. He is most anxious to meet you. Be advised he is a widower and very wealthy. His only son died last year and he needs a wife to get himself another heir. Wear your finest dress, niece and you may be fortunate!'

Lucy's stomach plummeted. Tobias was losing no time in trying to marry her off and giving no thought to her own needs and desires. Then she remembered Kate was coming after noon to help her move the goods. She had never been in the cellars or the cave. How much smuggled goods were there? Could two women move it? It might be too heavy? She felt panic rising, then realised Tobias was speaking again.

'It would be inappropriate for you to attend Lord Huntingdon's unescorted, so I have arranged for a widowed lady, Mrs Sophia Chadwick to accompany us. She has agreed to live here at High Ridge until such time you are married.'

'Is that really necessary, Tobias?' Her heart was sinking with every minute. 'I have been here over a month now and I've gone into Falcombe alone; ridden on the moors and beach. Why the sudden need for a chaperone?'

'We must comply with convention or your reputation will be irreparably damaged and no-one will want to marry you apart from a lowly person.'

'Well, perhaps I would be happier with a lowly person, than marry someone rich who I am miserable with!' she exclaimed.

'Nonsense!' he tutted. 'How could you be miserable with riches, which you would have if you marry Lord Huntingdon!'

'Will it make any difference if I say I do not need a chaperone?'

'None at all, niece.' He fixed her with a steely stare. 'Now go and choose your prettiest dress for this evening.'

Lucy went, tears of frustration spilling on to her cheeks. Why was Tobias curtailing the freedom she'd enjoyed since arriving in Cornwall? She had not given him any reason to.

Later that morning, Tobias left for Falcombe in the carriage. Now there was only Elvira to leave and the coast would be clear to begin the work of moving the goods.

Lucy was in the kitchen, giving instructions to Lizzie when Elvira walked in attired in her outdoor clothes. Her cold gaze flickered over Lucy.

'The master informed me he will return later this afternoon, Miss Armitage.' She thrust the set of household keys into Lucy's hand without further comment and left.

Lucy made her way to the rear door and walked to the Folly steps. Thankfully the tide was well out, but there was no sign of Kate and it had gone past the prearranged time. Had Jack discovered Kate's intentions and forbade her to come? The keys jangled in her pocket and she decided to go to the cellar and see how much room there was to store the smuggled goods.

Lucy unlocked the cellar door, entered with a lighted candle and locked the door behind her. The smell of damp mustiness was strong as she descended the steps into the cellar. The shelves and racks were stacked full of bottles of spirits — French brandy, rum and whisky. And there were dozens of bottles of wine.

She moved farther to the back of the cellar. There was a large empty area where the contraband could be stored. Beyond that was another stout wooden door. She tried several keys and finally found the one which unlocked it.

Lucy stared into the black void, suddenly nervous at stepping into the unknown alone. She took a deep breath and holding her candle high began to descend the path towards the cave. The tang of ocean and seaweed was strong and several times her candle nearly blew out from the breeze which came from the sea.

At last the path widened out into a

cave. About six feet up was a ledge with steps cut into the rock to reach it. Her heart sank as she realised the task before her. She counted them. Twenty large casks and as many bundles which she supposed was fabric and lace. Even with Kate's help it would take them all their time and energy to move them.

Lucy walked on and shortly emerged into the cave where the smugglers kept their boat. She walked out of the cave and stared along the beach. In the distance Kate was hurrying towards her.

'I'm sorry, Miss Armitage.' Kate said breathlessly as she reached her. 'It was Jack kept me. I couldn't get away and I durst tell him I was going to help you move the stuff.'

'Well, you're here now. We must hurry! There is more of it than I imagined!'

When they went into the cave, Kate suggested they tackle the barrels first. She was a lot sturdier than Lucy and appeared to make light work of humping them down the steps then rolling them to the cellar. Lucy found it back breaking work. The casks made a hollow echoing sound and Lucy realised that was the sound she had heard the night she'd mistaken it for the sea crashing into the cave.

After four barrels, Lucy had to rest. Kate shrugged her shoulders when asked to do the same.

'I've had to work hard most of my life, Miss. I'll rest when we've finished the barrels.'

Lucy felt obliged to carry on. It seemed an age before they finished and all the casks were lined neatly in the cellar.

'Can't do the rest now, Miss. I have to get back to my mother's and Jack'll wonder where I am if I'm not back before him.'

'Can you come back tonight, Kate, at ten? I have to attend a social evening at Lord Huntingdon's manor, but I'm going to pretend faintness and return home early.'

'Be careful, I've heard of Lord Huntingdon. He's got a bad reputation and if he gets his eye on you . . . ' Kate left unsaid the unsavoury aspect of Lord Huntingdon's aspirations.

'I have every intention of turning his attention from me, Kate.' Lucy answered in a determined tone. Arranging for Kate to return to the house that night at ten, the two women parted.

Lucy locked the cellar and went to her room to rest for an hour. She was dreading the evening ahead, especially being under the watchful eye of Mrs Sophia Chadwick! Later, with her dress for the evening ready, Lucy joined Tobias in the parlour for early tea.

'Mrs Chadwick will arrive later to accompany us, my dear. I do trust you will act civil towards her?'

'I am not at odds with her, personally, Tobias. I just think it is unnecessary when you will be with me.'

'I will not be with you the whole evening. The gentlemen have their own entertainment for part of the time.'

I'm certain the gaming table will be part of that entertainment, thought Lucy. She knew it was pointless to protest further so when the meal was over she excused herself to get ready for the evening.

Mrs Sophia Chadwick arrived promptly at seven-thirty. She was a bustling, plump woman with a no nonsense attitude. Tobias offered her a glass of his best port while they waited for Lucy to appear.

'I do hope your niece is not a flighty piece?' Sophia Chadwick asked. 'I've chaperoned young ladies before and dear me what a time I've had keeping some of them in check. Strict discipline is what they need!' She sniffed in a disapproving manner.

Tobias fixed his gaze on the mass of pink feathers attached to her silk turban. He almost burst out laughing, but with great effort kept his expression bland.

'I can assure you, my dear Mrs Chadwick, my niece, Lucy is not of a frivolous nature.'

At that moment, Lucy entered at Tobias' call. She was wearing an evening coat of silver brocade and a bonnet to match. Sophia Chadwick subjected her to a thorough examination from top to toe. After introductions, Sophia gave Lucy a lecture on the obligations of a young lady in polite society.

Lucy came quickly to the conclusion the woman was full of her own self importance. The trivial constant chatter all the way to the manor grated on Lucy so much she felt like screaming. Tobias appeared as irritated as she felt. Was he regretting his choice of chaperone?

The carriage turned into a wide curved drive as light as day with dozens of lanterns placed at intervals leading to the house, which was ablaze with light from every window.

'Oh, isn't this magnificent!' Sophia enthused as they alighted from the carriage and walked through the porticoed entrance and entered a hall so ostentatious even Sophia seemed over-awed by it.

Lucy had never seen so many chandeliers in one room and when they were shown into a ballroom even larger than the hall and saw the place was crowded with splendidly attired guests she began to have misgivings about what she had done! Her heart sank even further when across the room her gaze collided with Marcus' sardonic expression.

He looked darkly handsome in black, relieved only by the pristine white neck cloth and Lucy felt her heart begin to race. Then he turned away to give his attention to the woman by his side. She was breathtakingly beautiful with hair the colour of gold. Lucy felt a pang of jealousy. She realised Marcus would never look at her in that way.

Sophia was tugging on her arm. 'Come, Lucy. The ladies have a special room where we can leave our outer clothing and bonnets.'

'I think I'd rather keep mine on!' Lucy replied lamely.

'Nonsense! You'll faint with the heat, girl!'

They were shown to an ante room where a servant was waiting to take their coats. Sophia removed her coat to reveal the high-waisted gown she wore in white muslin with a satin under gown. The style was much too young for her and made her appear unbecoming.

Lucy tentatively removed her bonnet. Sophia gave her a glance, then turned to stare more fully at Lucy's tightly drawn back hair with not a curl in sight.

'Oh, dear me! Couldn't you have made more effort with your hair? It looks very plain.'

'I cannot do anything with it myself.' Lucy explained.

'Haven't you a maid to help you?' Sophia looked aghast.

Taking a deep breath, Lucy removed her coat.

Sophia's mouth dropped open. 'Oh, that will never do! Oh dear me no!' She stared at Lucy's grey plain linen gown in horror. 'Surely you have a more suitable gown for social events like this?'

The censure in her tone suddenly angered Lucy. She didn't care anymore what anyone thought, least of all Sophia Chadwick. She was wearing her old gown for a reason.

'There is nothing wrong with my gown! At least it is respectable which is more than can be said for some in there!' She marched towards the door, her head held high.

'You can't go in there dressed like that!' Sophia hissed.

'Why ever not? I'm perfectly decent!' Lucy countered and marched out.

Heads turned and conversation petered out as Lucy wandered through the ballroom looking for Tobias. She was aware Sophia was hanging back, ashamed to be associated with her. Good, thought Lucy, if she stayed away all night it would suit her. The woman was insufferable!

She turned to see Tobias walking towards her with a hugely obese middle-aged man whose rotund stomach protruded through his satin waistcoat.

She registered with a sinking heart the different emotions crossing her uncle's face. Shock, disgust and deep anger. However he kept his rage in check as he introduced her to Lord Percy Huntingdon.

'My dear, Miss Armitage I'm delighted to meet you.' Percy bowed low over her hand. Despite his polite words his monocle dropped from his eye as he took in her appearance. Lucy repressed a shiver. She did not fail to notice he too had anger in his own narrowed gaze. He was obviously expecting someone very different and she wondered just what Tobias had led him to believe. One thing she was sure of, if he was the last man on earth she wouldn't want to marry him!

'Perhaps we may become better acquainted later in the evening, Miss Armitage,' he said, but already his gaze was dismissive and his little pig-like eyes were roving the room, seeking elsewhere.

Lucy wanted to cheer. Her plan was

working perfectly. Hopefully there would be no more invitations to Ledley Manor. Lord Huntingdon might be easy to deal with, but one glance at Tobias and the cold fury in his eyes warned her she would not get away from his undoubted wrath!

'You will explain yourself when we return home as to the meaning of this charade!' he snapped as Percy Huntingdon moved away, then he also turned abruptly and left her.

Sophia appeared to have given up her chaperone duties. She was sitting with a group of other middle-aged ladies, chattering away, apparently conveniently forgetting her charge. A footman with a tray of drinks offered one to Lucy, which she took gratefully.

Very soon she would pretend a faint and return home to move the last of the smuggled goods.

'I observed you were trying very hard to impress our genial host!' The suave tones cut into her thoughts. Lucy looked up to meet Marcus' amused gaze.

'I would never want to impress that man!' she exclaimed vehemently.

'Obviously or you would not be playing this little game,' he chuckled, eyeing the plain linen gown with distaste.

'Tobias was determined Lord Huntingdon would find me a suitable candidate to be his next wife. I was equally determined he would not find me suitable by appearing as ugly and as plain as I could!'

His amused expression faded. 'You will never be plain or ugly, little Yorkshire miss!'

Lucy was taken aback by his sudden compliment and there was a look in his eyes which sent her heart soaring. Then he was holding out his arm, 'May I have the privilege of the next dance,' he asked.

'Oh, I couldn't possibly,' she replied. 'I haven't danced for a long time. I've forgotten the steps. Besides, I would not want to upset your companion of the evening.'

'My companion, as you put it is otherwise occupied.' He indicated to where the blonde woman was in conversation with one of the guests.

'Come, I will show you the steps and refresh your memory,' he insisted, but before they reached the dance area, Tobias was pushing his way forcefully through the guests towards them, his expression dark with fury.

'Trenarren! I would prefer it if you found some other female to flatter. My niece is not for the likes of you!'

'I happen to prefer your niece's company at the moment.' Marcus replied in a cold tone.

'Stay away from her Trenarren! I saw you sniffing around her on the beach. I dictate who she keeps company with!'

The two men eyed each other aggressively. Lucy was fearful it would end in violence.

'You cannot treat Lucy as you did my sister!' Marcus shouted out.

'I loved your sister! She wanted for nothing!'

'True enough until you found something you loved more! Your devotion to the gaming tables! Then Penelope suffered not only physical discomfort as you sold off everything to feed your habit, but humiliation also!'

Lucy, listening to the claims and counter claims of the two men realised someone had to put a stop to it. She put a hand to her head and swayed before crumpling to the floor.

Everyone nearby gathered round in morbid curiosity.

'Stand back!' Tobias snapped. 'Give the girl some air! Someone bring water!' Marcus gently lifted her into his arms and carried her to a chaise-longue near to a window which he opened.

Lucy moaned in the pretence of coming round. 'What happened?' she whispered.

'You fainted,' Marcus said and gently pushed her back as she tried to sit up. 'Lie still for a few minutes.'

At that moment, Tobias and Sophia walked up. 'Here, drink this.' Tobias handed Lucy a glass of water. For the time being his anger appeared to have abated.

She sipped it slowly. 'I don't feel well, Tobias. May I go home?'

'Of course, my dear. I'll organise the carriage for you. It can return for me later.'

So far, so good, thought Lucy. Tobias' next words had her wondering how on earth she was going to complete the task Jack had set her to do?

'Mrs Chadwick will accompany you home. We don't want you fainting again and no-one there to help you! Elvira is away tonight.'

Lucy stared at him. It seemed her well laid plans were crumbling! She had to think fast!

9

I shall accompany you home, Miss Armitage in my own carriage.' Marcus announced in a firm tone. Lucy glanced at Tobias who was frowning deeply.

'No you will not! I do not trust you, Trenarren!'

Marcus eyed him with contempt. 'I trusted you with my sister and look what happened! Miss Armitage will be quite safe with me.'

'No-one need put themselves out!' Lucy exclaimed. 'I will go home alone. Lizzie the maid will look after me.' She looked at Sophia. 'Please stay, Mrs Chadwick and enjoy the evening.'

'Well, I don't know,' she said flustered and turned to Tobias for support, but he had crossed the room to where Lord Huntingdon was watching proceedings.

'If you're quite sure.' Sophia began to

capitulate. 'It is a shame to leave such a marvellous party.'

Lucy lay back and closed her eyes, feeling a wave of relief, but there was still Marcus to contend with. Still, he was only offering to take her home and would not be staying. Once he had gone she could set to when Kate arrived and move the remaining bales with her.

'My carriage is waiting to take you home, Lucy.' The quiet voice spoke near her ear. She opened her eyes to see Marcus bending over her.

'Tobias will not be agreeable to you taking me home, Marcus.'

'I have persuaded him otherwise. Do you feel well enough to walk?' he asked.

'Yes, I think so,' she said, allowing Marcus to help her from the couch.

Tobias was standing at the entrance as they left the ballroom. His lips were tight with anger. 'Compromise my niece in any way and you will have me to deal with, Trenarren!' he spat out.

'She is safer with me than anyone in

Falcombe, especially Huntingdon who you are so desirous of shackling her to! Go to your gaming table, Penmarick!' Marcus answered harshly before leading Lucy to his carriage.

'You really had no need to put yourself out, Marcus.' Lucy turned to him once they were settled in the vehicle and it began to move along the brightly-lit drive. 'It was just a mere faint. It was so stuffy in there.'

Marcus looked down his aquiline nose at her with a shrewd expression. 'A mere faint was it? I would suggest it was a well planned act, time to perfection.'

Lucy stared at him. She realised he was very astute and not easily fooled. 'Very well, yes it was a pretend faint. Your argument with my uncle was becoming very heated. I had to stop you both or Lord knows where it would have ended.'

Marcus laughed softly. 'Thank you for your concern, but it wasn't the conversation which troubled you. I observed early on you appeared not to be enjoying the evening and wanted an excuse to be gone.'

'Again you are very observant, Marcus. As I have said before, Tobias was hoping to pair me off with Lord Huntingdon. Now I have met the man the thought of marriage to him makes me quite ill.'

'I would not allow your uncle to marry you off to that vain, foppish toad. I'd kill him myself first!' he exclaimed vehemently.

'There will be no need for such extreme violent measures,' Lucy replied, surprised by his outburst. 'I have no intention of marrying Lord Huntingdon!'

The tension in the close confines of the carriage was palpable. Before she could draw back or resist he bent forward and pulled her towards him. His cool lips closed over her own in a firm kiss and she was too stunned to draw away. At length he released her.

'Marcus, you promised my uncle!' she exclaimed.

His expression showed amusement.

'Now what did I promise your redoubtable uncle? I promised I wouldn't ravish you, which I believe Tobias thought I had in mind. He said nothing about an innocent little kiss. Did it offend you?'

Lucy stared into his eyes. The moonlight was casting its silver gleam into the coach, making his features appear like marble. 'No, it did not. It was just unexpected, that's all.'

'Well, I was robbed of a dance with a beautiful woman, despite the gown, so I deserve some reward for seeing Cinderella home.'

Lucy found herself joining Marcus in laughter at his remark. Further conversation was light and before long the carriage had reached High Ridge.

'I shall make certain you are safely inside before I return to Ledley Manor.' Marcus insisted.

The door opened and Lizzie emerged. 'Oh, Miss Lucy. I did not expect you back so early. I haven't got your bed ready or anything . . . ' Her voice faded into silence.

'No need to fret, Lizzie. I've returned home early as I fainted, but I feel a little better now. All I require is my bed turned back and warmed then you may go to bed yourself.'

The maid bobbed a curtsey. 'Very well, Miss.' She disappeared into the house.

'Thank you for accompanying me home, Marcus. Lizzie will look after me if I need anything.'

'As if you need it!' His tone was sarcastic.

Lucy chose to ignore his remark. 'I'm sure you are anxious to return to Lord Huntingdon's.'

'Am I? Now your gracious presence is no longer there, it will be dark without the light of your smile.'

'I do not think so somehow. I will say goodnight for to be truthful I am rather tired.'

Marcus bent low over her head, his keen gaze scanning her features. 'I will bid you goodnight then and hope there are no more fainting fits.' His cool lips touched her fingers.

As she turned to enter the house she was unaware of the calculating expression on his features.

Lucy locked the door and listened to Marcus' carriage recede into the distance. She opened the parlour door and moved to the fireplace. By the light of the fire which still burned dully in the hearth, she saw the small ornate mantel clock showed the hour was nine-thirty. She made her way to her bedroom where Lizzie was placing a bedpan warmer inside the bed, filled with hot ashes from the fire.

When the maid had gone, Lucy waited until she returned from downstairs and she heard her footsteps clatter up the uncarpeted stairs to the top floor where her room was allocated.

By now it was eight minutes to ten and Lucy quietly left her room and made her way downstairs to let Kate in. She unlocked the rear door and walked towards the Folly steps. She had no idea by what means Kate would travel to High Ridge, but as yet there was no sign of her.

A cool wind had sprung up and she drew her shawl closer around her body. Where was Kate? It must be after ten now, she thought after waiting several minutes. Perhaps Jack had discovered her intention? She couldn't wait any longer. She would have to try and complete the task herself.

Closing her hand over the cold metal of the cellar key in her pocket, she went back into the house to find a lantern. Descending the cellar steps, Lucy suddenly felt her courage failing. What was she doing anyway? If all the contraband was found in the cellar by the excise men, Tobias would be in serious trouble.

On the other hand, she could not risk a fourteen-year-old boy facing the hangman's noose. When Tobias discovered Jack had dumped the contraband in the cellar he would not risk his own neck surely by condemning those men?

She climbed to the shelf the bales

were stored on and set to, pushing each bale over to the floor below. Some were smaller than others and she was able to lift and carry them to the cellar. Unaccustomed to hard labour her arms and back were soon aching. There was one remaining to deal with when she became aware of the strengthening wind blowing through the cave.

The sea sounded much nearer than before and she realised the tide was coming in. She left the last bale and walked to the outer cave, stepping back quickly when her shoes became wet. In a short while both inner and outer caves would be flooded. She went back to drag the last bale up to the cellar, where she found the door closed. She knew she had left it open to save time.

She lifted the latch and pushed, but it wouldn't open. Putting all her weight behind it she pushed again. A cold hand touched her heart. Someone must have locked the door from the other side!

A chill of fear gripped her at the

thought she was trapped here in the freezing cold with the sea relentlessly pouring in! How far did the water reach? Surely not beyond the second cave or an opening with a door would not have been constructed when the house was built? With that thought she tried to comfort herself. She tried hammering on the door and shouting for help, but eventually she was too exhausted and gave up.

If Tobias had discovered the smugglers were trying to trap him into releasing their friends he would lose no time in disposing of the goods. Perhaps he was hoping whoever was down here would drown when the tide came in? She was quickly learning her uncle had a ruthless streak.

The time passed slowly and eventually she must have dozed because she suddenly awoke, aware of a lapping sound. She held the lantern out and saw the sea was only feet away! For a long time she watched the water creep nearer, then thankfully it remained mere inches away from the bale she was huddled on.

To add to her ordeal the candle burnt to nothing and she was plunged into mind-numbing pitch blackness. She struggled to quell the rising feeling of suffocation. She had always been terrified of the dark, but this was something else! Not a chink of light anywhere to focus her sight on. At that moment all she wanted was to be safe in Marcus' arms, but he didn't know she was here in this dark prison!

Drawing her thick cloak around her shivering body she lay on the bale and closed her eyes against the infinite darkness. Sleep came eventually, then she awoke, having no idea how long she had slept. Her arms and legs were cramped and she knew she had to get up and move about to dispel the deathly cold invading her body.

She could no longer hear the sea, and groping her way down the slope she felt her way along the tunnel, feeling along the slimy wet sides to give her an indication when she reached the cave. Gradually the blackness gave way to grey and she could see the outline of the tunnel. With profound relief she reached the outer cave and ran forward to the opening, gulping deep breaths of air.

It was a beautiful sunny day and judging by the sun still early. She began to walk towards the headland and was in sight of the Folly steps when she noticed a rowing boat coming in to shore. Further out was a lugger with its square sail. It lay still in the water, waiting presumably for the men in the rowing boat. They were jumping out and dragging it up the beach when Lucy suddenly recognised it was Jack and another man.

It was too late to try and hide even if she'd wanted to. They had already seen her and Jack was running towards her, shouting angrily.

Lucy didn't wait, she took to her heels and ran awkwardly through the sand. She hesitated only briefly as she reached the Folly steps. It was fear that gave her the impetus to hurry up the twisting, narrow steps, knowing the smuggler was only yards behind her. She stumbled over the hem of her skirt and nearly fell, but Jack had caught up and she recoiled as his arm fastened around her waist.

'Don't touch me!' she cried. 'I've done enough of your dirty work and that is the last time I do!'

'Stop struggling. I'm not going to harm you. Did you do as I told you?'

'Yes, damn you, I did and got locked in those caves all night for my trouble. Someone was hoping I'd drown!'

Jack grinned. 'Well I'm thinking it might have been your poxy uncle. He would do that if he thought it was me and the lads moving the stuff. Come on, you're coming for a little sea journey with me. I have to have something to bargain with if my first plan to free the lads doesn't work. You showed up at the right time.' He forced her back down the steps on to the beach.

He turned to his companion. 'Sam, check she's done the job.'

'Where is Kate?' Lucy asked as Sam hurried off to the cave.

'Safe enough. I found out about your little plan to get her to help you. I caught her creeping out the house last night. I say what she does and doesn't do!' He pulled her to the rowing boat and ordered her to get into it. She struggled and attempted to run, but Jack lifted her into his arms and dumped her into the boat.

'Try anymore tricks and I'll tie you up and gag you,' he snarled.

Before long, Sam returned. 'No stuff there now, only one bale near the cellar door.'

'Never mind that, as long as most of it is in Penmarick's cellar. Help me push this boat out.'

'Where are you taking me?' Lucy asked, struggling to sit up and pushed down by Sam's boot in her chest. They ignored her question as they concentrated on rowing to the lugger.

Lucy felt sick with fear, wondering what they were going to do to her. Her stomach was churning with hunger and her mouth dry with thirst. They heaved to by the side of the larger boat and Lucy was dragged aboard by a man she hadn't seen before. The rowing boat was tied to the lugger and the larger vessel was soon slicing through the water.

Lucy became more and more concerned as the dry land receded into the distance.

'We'll land ashore in Pengelly Bay,' Jack said.

They were rounding a headland when suddenly, as if from nowhere a much larger vessel came into view. 'It's the *Adelaide*.' Jack cursed. 'We can't hope to outrun her!'

Lucy heaved herself up on to her elbows. An imposing black-painted ship was ploughing with swift ease through the waves towards them. She could see it carried a red flag with the Union in one corner, but couldn't make out the other sign on it. What she could see was the gun ports in its bulwarks.

'What ship is it?' she asked.

'Don't you know?' Jack sneered. 'The *Adelaide* is a King's cutter and she's heading straight for us! Don't worry, she can't follow us much farther. The water's too shallow where we're going.'

To Lucy's untrained eye it seemed the Revenue ship would catch up long before they reached Pengelly Bay. It was gaining with every minute; its bow cutting through the white foam with amazing speed. Now it was nearer she could see its crew running about on the deck. Someone began shouting to them, but the words were carried away by the wind. The lugger was nearing the shore of Pengelly Bay and it was clear the *Adelaide* could come no farther as a small boat was being lowered over the side.

Quickly transferring from the lugger to the rowing boat, the three men soon reached the shore.

'What are we going to do with her?'

the man called Toby asked as they reached the beach and jumped out into the shallow water. 'She'll only hold us up.'

'She goes where we go!' Jack said firmly. 'Penmarick will pay good money to get her back!'

Suddenly a shot rang out! Then a second shot and Toby fell to the ground.

Jack took a firm grip on Lucy's arm and dragged her up the beach to a path leading to the top of the cliffs. For Toby he didn't give a second glance to see whether he was dead or alive. Sam followed close on their heels, fighting to get his breath as they reached the top.

'Lucy!' The shout came loud and clear from the beach. Lucy turned her head, recognising Marcus.

'Marcus!' she sobbed his name. Below them was a crowd of Revenue men and among them she picked out Marcus and Tobias.

Jack was also staring down at them

and Lucy was unprepared for his swift action when he produced a pistol from the belt at his waist. She tried to knock his arm away, but he took aim and fired!

10

The explosion from Jack's pistol was deafening in Lucy's ear. Then she saw the men below were crowding round a body. Someone had been hit!

'I do believe I've hit your dear uncle,' Jack smirked.

'No!' Lucy cried. Her gaze searched the huddle of men. 'Let me go to him, please? He may be seriously injured!'

'I sincerely hope the old blackguard's dead! He's determined to see Ben and the others hang, but it will be his funeral that will be arranged!'

'Let Miss Armitage go free and we will not deal harshly with you!' Marcus shouted up to them.

'She's staying with me, of her own choice!' Jack shouted back.

'Why did you say I was with you by my own choice!' Lucy demanded to know as Jack pulled her away from the cliff top.

'If we're to hang for all this, so will you. Now keep quiet and run,' Jack ordered. She found it hard to keep up with Jack's swift pace and many times she stumbled, only to be dragged to her feet again. Before long she was exhausted, not just with the exertion, but lack of water and food. She could hear Sam was finding it hard too. He was getting on in years and his breathing was becoming laboured as he tried to keep up.

'I don't think I can go much further, Jack!' he panted.

'Slow down and you're a dead man! We have to reach Ma's before them Revenue men sees us. Come on!'

Before long they were hurrying through the still quiet streets to a house set back from the main thoroughfare. Jack barged his way through the door without knocking.

'Ma! Where are you?' Jack opened a door through which Lucy could see a flight of stairs.

'No need to shout! I'm coming.'

Elvira answered, then her feet could be heard on the landing and descending the stairway. She appeared through the door and her whole expression changed when her eyes alighted on Lucy.

'What's she doing here. I thought I'd taken care of her!' Elvira's eyes were like dark pools of malevolence in her pinched features.

'Never mind her, Ma. We've no time to lose! The Revenue men are on our tail! We're going to hide in Sampson's mine till tonight. We need food and ale and be quick as you can!'

'What was she doing moving that stuff last night? I wanted her out of the way, that's why I locked her down there.'

'She was moving it on my orders to stop Penmarick hanging those men. If he's hiding contraband then he can't condemn anyone else.'

Elvira looked horrified. 'You can't implicate Tobias! He could hang as well as those men!'

Jack gave a mirthless chuckle. 'That's

right, Ma. He knows I'll squeal on him if he hangs Ben. Now hurry up with that food!'

Elvira's complexion turned grey with horror. 'I don't care about the others anymore. Tobias is the only person who matters to me after you, Jack.'

'Well you'll just have to forget him, Ma. I shot him and I hope he's dead!'

'You've shot him? Why? He was protecting us and paying good money for the stuff you brought from France!'

'He's turned traitor, Ma. In with Marcus Trenarren and the Riding Officer.'

Elvira's stricken gaze slid to Lucy. 'It's because of you! If you hadn't come here to Cornwall things would have gone on the same and Tobias would have married me, he more or less promised it would happen one day. High Ridge would have been mine! You've spoiled everything! It was a high tide last evening and I was hoping you would drown!'

'Thankfully it wasn't high enough,

Elvira,' Lucy replied in a sarcastic tone. 'Now I understand why you resent my presence at High Ridge. I can tell you now, Tobias has no intention of marrying again.'

'Come on, you two.' Jack interrupted. 'The Revenue men are on our tail and just like women you stand arguing about a man!'

Elvira sent Jack an angry look, but began to spread a large cloth on the table and went to a cupboard, from which she brought out a loaf of bread, cheese and ale. She hurriedly cut the loaf into thick slices and tied the food in the cloth before handing it to Jack.

'You won't see me for a while after tonight, Ma. Sailing on the *Merry Maid* to France till things quieten down.'

'What about her?' she asked, her hostile glare turning to Lucy.

'She's coming with me, who knows we may even wed!' he joked.

'No! Not with her!' Elvira looked aghast. 'Why don't you bargain with Trenarren. He'll pay good money for her,' she suggested.

'Now that's a good idea,' Jack said, stroking his chin thoughtfully. 'Trouble is my neck can feel that rope tightening already. I may have to bargain my way out of England so I'll keep this fine lady as my ship's ticket.' He placed his arm around Lucy's waist and drew her close.

'There's no way of knowing what the time is down in that place, Ma. Will you promise to come and stand a little way into the tunnel entrance after dark about an hour before the ship sails. Bring a lantern and hold it high. I'll keep looking out for it. But for Heaven's sake keep an eye out for them Revenue men!'

'I don't like going anywhere near that place, son, especially at night, but I'll do it for you.'

They left the house and Sam turned to go the opposite way. 'There's no way I'm going down Sampson's mine, Jack. I'll hide in Dan's tavern cellar until tonight.'

'Be it on your own head, or neck if they catch you.' Jack laughed coarsely, fingering his own neck.

'Come, little lady. We're going to keep each other company in the dark,' he chuckled.

The wind blew across the open moorland, waving the gorse like a restless sea. Ahead the large wheel of the mine stood out in stark contrast to the beautiful countryside. The old ruin appeared to be teetering on the edge of the cliff as they hurried towards it. Jack kept scanning the path behind them for sight of the Revenue men.

'Why do people think it's haunted?' Lucy asked, feeling a tinge of trepidation herself.

'The mine was in use for decades, but was abandoned a few years ago when there was a landfall and part of the shaft caved in. The only one killed was Josiah Sampson, all the other men got out alive. Josiah's body was never recovered. Strange noises have been heard coming from deep within the bowels of the place. Some say it's Josiah calling for help. Are you afraid, little lady?' he mocked.

'No, not of any supposed ghost, but I am afraid of dark, enclosed places. Surely there must be a better place to hide?' She hung back as the black entrance to the tunnel came into view.

'Well that's just too bad?' Jack sneered. 'My neck's more important than your silly fears!' he pushed her forcefully towards the tunnel.

The interior of the tunnel was damp and there was a constant eerie dripping sound. A weird wailing noise rattled along the tunnel, causing the hairs on the back of Lucy's neck to stand on end.

'That's only old Sampson complaining at being disturbed,' he laughed.

Jack stopped and began to feel along the top of the wall and brought down a lantern and a tinderbox. Within a minute or two the candle in the lantern was lit.

'How far in are we going?' she asked.

'I need something to eat and drink.'

'Not far. There's a storage place we can stay in,' he replied.

They walked further on through a narrow tunnel, then it suddenly widened out. Jack stopped and in the dim light Lucy could see there was an iron door set in the wall.

'We used to hide the stuff down here, but when Penmarick took over as leader he said we had to use the cave under High Ridge as Trenarren had found out we hid our loot here. Your uncle's a traitor and if I haven't killed him, someone will for betraying us to the Revenue. Get in there and keep your mouth shut!' he said in a threatening tone.

Barrels and sacks were stacked in a corner, but there was also a table, two chairs and a truckle bed.

'Marcus will not rest until he has searched every corner of Cornwall to find me and apprehend you to make certain you face punishment,' she said in a defiant tone, praying Marcus would think to search the mine.

Jack moved closer, scanning her features in the light from the lantern held near her face. 'On first name terms, are we?' he laughed coarsely. 'Hoping he'll come and rescue you? Don't pin your hopes on him. He's only interested in putting the noose round folks' necks, like Penmarick. If he does come here, I'll have this waiting for him!' He brandished the pistol near her face.

* * *

Marcus instructed a soldier to cover the dead body of Tobias Penmarick. Jack Malvern's aim had hit the magistrate squarely in the chest. The smuggler, now turned murderer would surely hang when caught. He would be pursued to hell and back now he held Lucy. If he harmed her Marcus swore he would kill him with his bare hands.

He realised how much Lucy had come to mean to him. For years he had searched for someone like her, with her refreshing innocence and honesty. It was going to be difficult extracting himself from the liaison he had with Lydia Baring-Summers, although as yet there was no formal engagement. Lydia's father would be the most difficult to placate. Lord Baring-Summers was anxious to see his daughter married to a wealthy man.

Marcus brought his mind back to the more urgent situation when he realised Matthew Cornby was approaching him. He tried to suppress the irritation he always felt when the Riding Officer spoke to him. The man was too pretentious for his own good.

'Sir, the dragoons are scouring the whole area and I am confident we'll apprehend the man who killed Mr Penmarick shortly.' Matthew Cornby spoke in a blustering manner.

'I sincerely hope so, Mr Cornby, for Miss Armitage's sake.' Marcus said, mounting his horse, anxious to be away. He wanted to be alone to think. He rode along until he reached the twisting narrow path snaking up the cliff. Where would Malvern go until he could make his escape by ship? Marcus was certain he would try to leave the country.

Then like divine inspiration he suddenly remembered the old disused tin mine in the area. Surely Malvern would not risk hiding down there? He knew there was an old tunnel which led into one part of the mine; built to act as an escape route when the mine was in use, but it was unsafe now. If that is where he had gone, Marcus felt sick to think of Lucy in that dangerous place!

Should he summon help from Matthew Cornby and his men, he wondered? No, this was something he had to tackle alone. He could deal with Jack Malvern. He stopped at a nearby hamlet to borrow a lantern, then spurring Spartan on he set off across the moor towards Sampson's mine.

Lucy had covered her shoulders with the thin threadbare blanket from the pallet bed. It was cold in here, but the bread and cheese provided by Elvira had warmed her to some degree. Jack had already drunk two bottles of ale and begun another.

'Will Elvira keep her promise and let us know when we can leave here?' Lucy asked.

'Of course she will. If my Ma promises something she will do it. Now get up and let me have a turn on that bed.'

She sprang swiftly from the bed as he lurched towards her and went to sit at the table. Hours seemed to pass, but as there was no way of gauging time it could have only been minutes. She rested her head on the table and dozed. When she awoke she glanced at Jack and saw he had dozed off. It was her chance to escape!

She picked up the lantern and slowly walked backwards to the door, keeping her eyes unwaveringly on the sleeping man. The door was stiff and heavy and creaked loudly as Lucy dragged it open. Jack awoke, but being half asleep she was through the door before he realised it and he lumbered awkwardly after her.

Lucy hurried along the tunnel until she tripped and dropped the lantern. She was left stumbling along in pitch darkness. She prayed Jack was too intoxicated to catch up with her, but her hopes came to nothing when an arm shot out and curled around her neck, forcing her back against his body.

'Fed up of my company, little lady?' Jack's arm tightened, restricting her breathing. 'You ain't going nowhere.' He began to force her back towards the storeroom.

'Let me go, you brute!' she cried, trying to twist out of his hold.

'Sssh! What's that noise,' Jack said.

'I can't hear anything,' she whispered. All she could hear was the drip drip of condensation running down the walls. Then, deep within the bowels came the hacking sound of someone with a pick axe working at a seam as they would have done years before when the mine was in use. The hairs rose on Lucy's neck! No mortal being could be down here working! Yet still the sound went on.

'I don't like this!' Jack had terror written on his features. 'I'm getting out of here!' He released his hold on Lucy and was about to run when she heard him gasp in terror. From out of the darkness a tall figure approached holding a high lantern.

'You will have to pass me first, Malvern.' The suave tones echoed along the tunnel.

'Marcus!' Lucy cried. She tried to run to him, but Jack had pulled himself together and he prevented her passing him.

'Let her go, Malvern. You know the game's up. There's no way you're going to get on that ship tonight.'

'You think not, Trenarren. We'll see about that! This little lady is my bargaining point. Let me go free and you can have her.'

'Don't be a fool man. I'll see you get a fair trial. Trying to escape will only make your case worse. I'll be presiding judge now in Penmarick's stead.'

'Is my uncle badly hurt?' Lucy asked in a quiet voice.

An expression of pity briefly crossed Marcus' features. 'I am so very sorry, Lucy. Tobias died instantly. His body has been taken back to High Ridge to rest.'

A sob rose in her throat. She had known her uncle for only a short time, but he was the last link to her mother and now she had no family left.

'He died a quick death. More than can be said for the men he hanged!' Jack sneered. 'Now get out of my way, Trenarren.' Jack suddenly drew a pistol from his belt.

'There's only one way out, Malvern and I'm standing in the way.' Marcus said. 'For God's sake use your head. If you fire that in here you could cause the whole place to collapse!'

'Move back, let us through and we'll all live!' Jack shouted.

'You are not taking Lucy. Let her go

and I'll allow you to escape!'

'I don't trust you, Trenarren.' Jack raised his pistol and without warning fired at Marcus.

'You fool!' Marcus ducked quickly out of the way. 'You'll have us all killed!'

The sound of the pistol being fired in the confined space was like the boom of a cannon. Shards of rock began to fall from the roof of the tunnel. Jack stared upwards as the fall became heavier. In that instance, Marcus ran forward and dragged Lucy from his hold.

'Run, as fast as you can!' he told her, catching hold of her hand. Jack fired at them again, but in the darkness his aim missed.

As they ran towards the opening of the tunnel, Lucy became aware of a loud thundering noise. Daylight was in sight when she realised Marcus was correct. The whole tunnel was caving in!

11

They emerged from the rapidly disintegrating tunnel into the dusk of evening, coughing and spluttering as clouds of dust followed in their wake spewing from the mouth of the mine. There was a tremendous roar, then an eerie deathly silence.

Lucy lay sprawled on the ground where she had fallen. After several minutes she tentatively lifted her head and ran her hand over her face to clear it of dust. Marcus was lying nearby, not moving. There was no sign of Jack.

'Marcus!' she called, struggling to her feet. She stumbled to him and saw he was unconscious. Fear gripped her heart. 'Marcus!' she said again and gently lifted his head, supporting it with her arm. Marcus moaned, sending a wave of relief through her. He opened his eyes and for a brief moment he looked puzzled, then he smiled.

'Lucy, thank God you are safe.' He glanced around. 'Malvern?'

'I don't think he escaped,' she said, turning her head to see the entrance of the tunnel was no longer a black gaping hole. Tons of rubble blocked the exit. It appeared Jack hadn't stood a chance. She didn't like the man, but it was a horrible way to die.

'I think something hit my head, as we came out?' Marcus gingerly touched his head where blood had congealed.

'Allow me to look at you,' she asked, concerned.

'Never mind me,' he said, struggling to sit up. 'What about you? Are you hurt?'

She shook her head, close to tears after her ordeal. Marcus reached for her and held her close. 'I would never have forgiven myself if anything had happened to you.'

His words sent a surge of hope through her. He did care about her! 'He could have killed you, Marcus!' she replied. 'Why did you come here alone without the soldiers?'

'I hadn't time. I knew of this tunnel and guessed it was the one place Malvern would know no-one, not even the Revenue men would care to search. The superstition of it being haunted is too strong. And bringing soldiers with the Riding Officer would only have angered Malvern further. I couldn't take the chance of him hurting you.'

She drew away and smiled. 'Were you trying to frighten him, making those noises. You certainly frightened me!'

'What noises? I assure you I hadn't time to play games.'

A shiver ran through Lucy. 'We both heard someone with a pickaxe working in the mine. How silly of me, it couldn't have been you. The sound came from deep within the bowels of the mine, but who . . . ' She stopped speaking. 'So it is not just superstition.'

'So you heard old Sampson hard at work,' he chuckled. 'Forget him, he can't harm anyone.' He rose rather unsteadily to his feet. 'On more serious matters, if you are agreeable I will make all the arrangements for laying your uncle to rest?'

'I could not ask you to take on the responsibility!'

'Nonsense!' He brushed aside her protestations. 'You have been through a very distressing time. Come with me to Craghill Hall and stay for a while. My housekeeper will look after you.'

A shadow of grief crossed her features. 'Thank you, but no, I must return to High Ridge. Although I would be grateful for your offer to make the arrangements for my uncle's funeral. Firstly I have another unpleasant task to do. I must visit Elvira and inform her of the accident in the mine.'

'I will inform her of the bad news,' Marcus stated in a firm tone. Giving a loud whistle, Spartan appeared from behind a clump of bushes. Lucy was helped into the saddle and Marcus swung himself up behind her.

On the way to Elvira's house, Lucy

wondered how she would take the news that her son had perished in the mine and Tobias, the man she loved, dead by her son's hand.

Elvira's expression was suspicious when she opened the door. 'What's happened? Where's Jack?'

'May I come in, Mrs Samuel,' Marcus asked. He didn't like the woman and knew of her activities aiding the smugglers, but now he felt only pity.

'No, you tell me here what you have to say. I know you won't be satisfied until my Jack is hanged.'

'I'm sorry to have to impart bad news, but there's been a cave-in at the mine where your son was hiding with Miss Armitage. He foolishly tried to shoot at me and the reverberations caused a landslide. He wasn't quick enough to get out.'

'But it appears she was!' Elvira's dark malevolent gaze turned to Lucy, who was standing some way off with Spartan.

Her complexion began to turn chalk white as the news of her son's death sank in. 'At least my son can't hang now,' she remarked in an acrid tone.

'I have more bad news, I'm afraid. Tobias died when your son shot at the Revenue men.'

Elvira stared at Marcus as if she hadn't heard him, then her features crumpled in a spasm of pain and grief; all her composure and defiance gone. Her legs began to give way and Marcus had to catch her before she fell. He helped her indoors on to a settle. He searched in the cupboards and found a bottle of brandy. He made Elvira take a good measure and watched as some colour returned to her face.

'I've no-one now. Jack and my work at High Ridge were my only means of support.' Her features were haggard. Gone was the cold, haughty demeanour. In its place a sad, grief-stricken middle-aged woman. 'My life is not worth living,' she added, a sob catching in her throat.

'You are bound to feel deep grief at

this time, Mrs Samuel, but it will pass. I will help you all I can.'

Tears began to roll down her cheeks. Marcus thought it best he leave her to cry out her grief. He moved towards the door, but she caught his sleeve. 'Tell Miss Armitage I'm sorry I was harsh towards her. I really did love her uncle.'

Marcus left, promising again he would not see her destitute.

'How did she take the news?' Lucy asked as he helped her mount Spartan.

'Quite badly, I'm afraid. She has just confided to me she has no-one now Jack has gone.'

Lucy was thoughtful as Marcus spurred his mount towards High Ridge. She could not spare any pity for Elvira at the moment. There were too many other pressing problems to occupy her mind, but something must be done for the woman. She could not bear grudges or see anyone in hardship.

After the ordeal of Tobias' funeral, Lucy tried in the following week to settle down to life as mistress of High

Ridge, but so much had happened in such a short space of time she felt restless and depressed after such a traumatic time.

Of Marcus she had seen very little. Today was the day when he was presiding, in place of Tobias, to judge the case of young Ben and the other men caught smuggling. Lucy had come to believe Marcus was a fair judge, but even he could not waiver the law of the land. He had promised when it was over to visit her to let her know the outcome and he had also intimated he had something important to discuss with her.

Molly was once again working at High Ridge and at Lucy's request had found her a spaniel puppy. The little dog was now running rings around her heels so she decided to take the animal, whom she had named Springer, for a walk on the beach.

A strong wind had sprung up during the morning and now towards evening dark clouds were gathering, threatening to erupt in a storm. Lucy gave Springer a few minutes to exercise, but when large spots of rain began to fall, she put the dog on his lead and hurried towards the house.

'There's a visitor for you, Miss, in the parlour.' Lizzie came to take Lucy's cloak as she entered the hallway.

'Oh, is it Mr Trenarren?' Lucy asked. Her heartbeat quickened at the thought of seeing him again.

'It's Mrs Samuel.' The maid gave a grimace as she had never liked Elvira.

'Very well, thank you, Lizzie. Take Springer to the kitchen and would you bring us a tray of tea and some of those lovely scones Molly bakes with butter, please.'

Elvira rose from the settle when Lucy entered the parlour. She appeared a menacing figure all in black. Lucy tried to stifle her dislike for the woman and replace it with sympathy.

'Lizzie will bring us tea in a moment. What can I do for you, Mrs Samuel?'

Elvira drew herself up. 'I haven't

come for tea, Miss Armitage. Only, with your permission to collect some personal possessions which I left in my room.'

'Of course you may. Go and collect them now and have some tea when you return. I wish to speak with you.' Lucy said.

Elvira rose to her feet and walked towards the door. At that same moment a flash of lightning lit the sky outside. She stopped at the door. 'It's turning into a wild night. The tide will be running high.' Her ominous words were echoed by a clap of thunder. Rain started to lash against the window.

'You may stay here until the storm abates if you wish, Mrs Samuel? All night if necessary.'

Elvira turned her black gaze to Lucy. For a moment, Lucy thought she saw a gleam of malice in her dark eyes, but the woman's next words dispelled that.

'That's very kind of you, Miss Armitage. I would like to take up your offer to stay for the night.' A thin smile curved her lips.

Lizzie brought the tea tray. Lucy asked her to make up Elvira's bed and put a warming pan in to air it.

A half-hour passed and Elvira had not returned. The tea was going cold and Lucy began to wonder how many possessions Elvira had to collect? She left the parlour and ascended the stairs to the housekeeper's old room. She tapped on the door, but receiving no answer she opened the door and got the shock of her life to see poor Lizzie bound hand and foot on the bed. Sam was tying a gag over her mouth.

'What on earth . . . ' Lucy exclaimed.

Elvira was standing at the window, staring out at the wild elements. She turned, a terrible smile on her harsh features. 'Good, you're here at last. Sam, tie her hands together. Now I can do what I have been planning since my Jack died.'

It was then, Lucy saw the pistol in her hand, pointing directly at her!

12

Lucy's shocked gaze was riveted on the weapon in Elvira's hand. Sam twisted her round and roughly tied a length of cord tightly around her wrists.

'Did you think I wouldn't avenge my son's death?' Elvira's voice was quiet, but cold with deadly menace.

'Will vengeance bring him back?' Lucy answered quietly. 'Jack brought about his own death.'

'If that interfering upstart, Trenarren hadn't gone searching for you, Jack would have been on that ship at midnight, away from the Revenue men. Now, we're going for a little walk down to the cellars.'

'You can't leave Lizzie like that!' Lucy cried.

'She'll be fine until Molly finds her in the morning.'

Lucy had no option but do as Elvira

ordered, knowing the pistol was trained on her back.

Where was Marcus? It was dusk and it would be dark shortly. Surely he would not still be in court? What was Elvira intending to do? Lucy could understand the woman's grief, but to blame her for the loss of her son was madness!

As they passed the rear door, Elvira told Sam to pick up the lantern they had brought with them. Springer was barking with excitement in the kitchen when he heard their voices, but the door was closed and the little dog couldn't get out. Sam led the way through the cellar, which had now been cleared of the contraband by the Riding Officer, Matthew Cornby.

When Sam opened the door leading to the cave, the icy blast took their breath away. The wind roared down the tunnel like a ferocious beast.

They reached the outer cave and Lucy saw the tide was coming in. 'What are you intending to do, Elvira. Marcus will visit anytime now and he is certain to look for me.'

'I hope it will be too late by then!' She gave a harsh laugh, glancing towards the sea. Sam began to tie the rope she was bound with to the metal ring used for anchoring the rowing boat. Elvira's words sent a chill of fear racing through Lucy as her meaning became horrible clear. The sea was rushing in and already halfway up the beach!

'For pity's sake, Elvira you can't leave me here with the tide coming in! Think what you are doing!' Lucy pleaded.

'I know what I am doing. High Ridge would have been mine, if you hadn't come here. Now no-one will have it. I'm left with nothing because of you! Goodbye Miss Armitage!'

'Bye little Miss,' Sam said, chuckling. 'Who knows that gentleman friend of yours might turn up.' After making sure Lucy was well secured they walked back to the cellar without a backward glance.

The water began to swirl around her ankles, icy cold and chilling her to the bone. The sound of the wild approaching ocean with the wind tearing at her hair and clothing only added to her torment. It was quite dark now with flashes of lightning lighting up the sky at intervals.

Her knees were submerged when in between the loud claps of thunder she heard a dog barking. Springer! It must be him! A sudden surge of hope rose in her. She began shouting his name. The high pitched yelping became louder.

'Springer!' Lucy shouted.

Then she heard another sound. A man's voice calling her name.

'Marcus, I'm here, in the cave!' Her voice was carried away by the wind and she wept in frustration.

A light wavered in the darkness. It was Marcus! He placed his lantern on the ledge and waded towards her.

'You're safe now, Lucy, my dearest.' His arms closed around her, bringing blessed comfort, then he was deftly untying the cords binding her wrists.

'Elvira did this, she . . . ' Lucy began to tell him.

'That does not surprise me. I never believed she was a changed woman, but no more talking for now or we'll both drown. Let's get you to somewhere warm and dry.' He gathered her up into his arms and carried her up the tunnel, through the cellars to the parlour. He lowered her on to the settle near the fire and poured a brandy. 'Drink all this,' he instructed.

The fiery liquid burned as Lucy sipped it. 'Elvira had that friend of Jack's helping her, he tied me up. She blamed me for Jack's death and has been planning revenge since it happened. They intended that I would drown!' She shivered at the thought of how close to death she had been. 'I was terrified you wouldn't come in time . . . '

'Hush now,' he said gently. 'It's over. Thank goodness for this little dog of yours. He ran straight to the cellar door when I let him out of the kitchen.'

'Elvira must be caught, Marcus. She is quite insane!'

'Don't worry, my love. They will both be caught and punished,' he stated grimly.

'Poor Lizzie is in Elvira's old room, bound hand and foot.'

'Very well, I'll go and find her while you stay here near the fire. Then she must help you out of those wet clothes before you get a chill.'

Lucy huddled near the fire once Marcus had gone thinking over all that had happened, then something he had said bubbled up in her mind.

He had called her, 'my love and my dearest'. Did he really think of her as his love? He had not yet said so.

Lizzie burst into the room at that moment. 'Oh Miss Lucy, are you all right? Did that evil woman harm you?'

'No, I have Mr Trenarren to thank for my life or I would have drowned. I will tell you all later.'

'Yes, indeed she will!' Marcus entered

the room. 'Just now she needs to get out of those wet clothes and a hot posset making, please Lizzie. I wish to speak with your mistress.'

Lizzie hurried to the kitchen.

'I can't thank you enough for saving my life, Marcus,' Lucy said as he seated himself on the settle beside her. He took her cold hands in his own strong warm ones.

'To have you here, my darling safe and well is all I ask. If you are not already aware, my dear Lucy, I love you and I want you to be my wife.'

Lucy stared into his eyes, wanting to be certain he wasn't teasing her. There was no glimmer of mockery, only tenderness and sincerity.

'I love you too, Marcus and I would be honoured to be your wife.' Lucy replied, the horror of the last hours dissipating into joyous happiness.

Marcus drew her close and gave her a lingering kiss. 'I think I've loved you since the moment I first saw you, my dearest, looking out of the coach window with your pert little nose turned up at me.'

'I think I also have loved you for almost as long, but I tried to suppress my feeling as I never believed you could ever love someone like me!'

'It's because of what you are, my dear that I love you!' he murmured tenderly.

'Why did you let me go on believing you were a smuggler?' she asked. 'When I first met you I thought you were plotting something with Watson to do with smuggling. I knew it wasn't the weather which caused me to have to spend the night at the inn.'

Marcus smiled. 'Watson was working for me. Call it spying if you like. I'm sorry it delayed your journey. I didn't want you to think the worst of me, but the night the Revenue men were combing the beach, I was waiting for a ship, bringing my brother, Clive home. He's a spy for the Government and has been in France for some months now.

'We think Napoleon Boneparte is coming to prominence again and may be a threat to this country. Thankfully Clive missed the ship or he may have been caught as a French spy.

'Unfortunately, Jack Malvern and his cronies were coming in with cargo at the same time. I thought it was Clive landing. It was only when I heard the Revenue men firing at them I realised I had to get away fast or they would have believed I was part of the gang. Thank goodness you were taking a walk and gave me shelter. Now, enough about my escapades I think it's time you let Lizzie look after you and I will call tomorrow when you have rested.'

'Before you go, Marcus what was the outcome of the trial today?' Lucy asked as he rose to his feet.

'The men are to be deported to the colonies. Ben is going to Bodmin jail. I'm sorry for the boy, but it is the most lenient sentence I could give them.'

'I don't believe my uncle would have been so lenient. He appeared to enjoy hanging people,' she murmured.

'I no more favour the gibbet than

you do, Lucy. But others are not so compassionate. Lord Huntingdon caused an uproar in court, denouncing my judgement. That's why I was delayed. He said I should have those men hanged! He knows my term as magistrate is temporary and seeks to fill the post. I will do all I can to see he does not!' he said vehemently.

'I never believed you would send them to the gibbet, Marcus. You are just and compassionate and that is why I love you.'

There was silence for several minutes as they affirmed their love again with a kiss.

'When we marry what will happened to High Ridge? I've come to love this place, despite the perilous time I've spent since coming here to live.' Lucy glanced around the parlour. Was it only two months since she first arrived, believing it would be for a short time.

'If you wish we can divide our time between both homes.'

Lucy nestled close to him, murmuring her agreement. She had come to Cornwall a stranger, thinking it folly to love this man, not realising he was her destiny and her only true love.

THE END

We do hope that you have enjoyed reading this large print book.

Did you know that all of our titles are available for purchase?

We publish a wide range of high quality large print books including:
Romances, Mysteries, Classics
General Fiction
Non Fiction and Westerns

Special interest titles available in large print are:
The Little Oxford Dictionary
Music Book, Song Book
Hymn Book, Service Book

Also available from us courtesy of Oxford University Press:
Young Readers' Dictionary
(large print edition)
Young Readers' Thesaurus
(large print edition)

For further information or a free brochure, please contact us at:
Ulverscroft Large Print Books Ltd.,
The Green, Bradgate Road, Anstey,
Leicester, LE7 7FU, England.
Tel: (00 44) **0116 236 4325**
Fax: (00 44) **0116 234 0205**

FINDING THE SNOWDON LILY

Heather Pardoe

Catrin Owen's father, a guide on Snowdon, shows botanists the sites of rare plants. He wants his daughter to marry Taran Davies. But then the attractive photographer Philip Meredith and his sister arrive, competing to be first to photograph the 'Snowdon Lily' in its secret location. His arrival soon has Catrin embroiled in the race, and she finds her life, as well as her heart, at stake. For the coveted prize generates treachery amongst the rivals — and Taran's jealousy . . .

KEEP SAFE THE PAST

Dorothy Taylor

Their bookshop in the old Edwardian Arcade meant everything to Jenny Wyatt and her father. But were the rumours that the arcade was to be sold to a development company true? Jenny decides to organise a protest group. Then, when darkly attractive Leo Cooper enters her life, his upbeat personality is like a breath of fresh air. But as their relationship develops, Jenny questions her judgement of him. Are her dreams of true love about to be dashed?